THE PRESIDENT AND ME:

★ ★ ★ ★ ★ ★ ★

JOHN ADAMS AND THE MAGIC BOBBLEHEAD

Deborah Kalb

4880 Lower Valley Road • Atglen, PA 19310

Other Schiffer Books by Deborah Kalb:

The President and Me: George Washington and the Magic Hat,
ISBN 978-0-7643-5110-5

Other Schiffer Books on Related Subjects:

Mr. President and The First Lady: The DC Eagle Cam Project by
Teena Ruark Gorrow and Craig A. Koppie in cooperation with the
American Eagle Foundation, ISBN: 978-0-7643-5360-4

Mystery of Mary Surratt: The Plot to Kill President Lincoln by
Rebecca C. Jones, ISBN: 978-0-87033-560-0

The United States Presidents Illustrated by Robert M. Reed, ISBN:
978-0-7643-3280-7

Copyright © 2018 by Deborah Kalb
Illustrations © 2018 by Robert Lunsford

Library of Congress Control Number: 2018937200

Designed by Jack Chappell
Cover design by Brenda McCallum
Type set in Bookman Old Style

ISBN: 978-0-7643-5556-1
Printed in China
Published by Schiffer Publishing, Ltd.
4880 Lower Valley Road
Atglen, PA 19310
Phone: (610) 593-1777; Fax: (610) 593-2002
E-mail: Info@schifferbooks.com
Web: www.schifferbooks.com

For our complete selection of fine books on this and related subjects, please
visit our website at www.schifferbooks.com. You may also write for a free catalog.

Schiffer Publishing's titles are available at special discounts for bulk purchases
for sales promotions or premiums. Special editions, including personalized covers,
corporate imprints, and excerpts, can be created in large quantities for special
needs. For more information, contact the publisher.

We are always looking for people to write books on new and related subjects. If
you have an idea for a book, please contact us at proposals@schifferbooks.com.

Dedication

To my husband, David Levitt,

and my son, Aaron Kalb Levitt,

wonderful companions on the Freedom Trail and beyond,

with much love.

Chapter ~1~

va had always enjoyed flying. That was a good thing, because when your mom lived in Maryland and your dad in California, you spent way too much time on airplanes. But one thing that always annoyed her was someone kicking the back of her seat. And that's what was happening now. Kick, kick, kick, accompanied by the extremely tiresome voice of her stepbrother, J.P.

"And the new version comes with a special Darth Vader mini-figure," he was saying to his dad, Ava's stepfather Steve. "I heard the new version is much better than the old one." Ava sighed and looked out the plane window. It wasn't as if she hated Legos, but J.P. was completely obsessed. She was just so sick of hearing about them. The plane, which had just departed from Washington National Airport bound for Boston, was making a wide turn, giving Ava a view mostly of clouds. "We have reached 10,000 feet," the flight attendant intoned. "You are now free to use approved portable electronic devices."

Kick, kick, kick. "Whoa, look at those clouds," J.P. was exclaiming. Ava could hear Steve murmuring something in reply. Her mom, next to her, was reading a book. Ava considered pulling out something to read from her own backpack, but decided instead to focus on the wedding. Her aunt's wedding was tomorrow, and Ava was a flower girl! It would have been better if J.P. hadn't been part of the wedding party, too, but she couldn't do anything about that.

Although she had tried. "Mom," she had argued, "I mean, I'm Aunt Suzanne's real niece, and J.P. isn't her real nephew." As usual, her mom had shut down that line of argument while being her reasonable, therapist self, understanding Ava's feelings but somehow unwilling to do what Ava wanted. Sometimes having a therapist for a mom was frustrating. Her dad was a little easier to deal with. He was a veterinarian, as was his wife, Eleanor, and they lived in Northern California, in a sprawling house with no step-siblings and lots of dogs. At her mom's, Ava had her beloved cat, Hermione, who was being cared for this weekend by Ava's equally beloved best friend, Samantha.

"I hope Samantha remembers to feed Hermione," Ava said. "I'm sure she will," her mom replied, looking up from her book. "She's been very reliable in the past." Kick, kick, kick. It was just too much.

"Stop it!" Ava hissed, glaring at J.P. around the corner of the seat.

"What? What's wrong?" J.P. asked, looking clueless. Honestly! Eight-year-olds shouldn't kick other people's seats!

"Stop kicking the seat! You're not a baby! Just stop it!"

Maybe she should have taken J.P. up on his offer to sit next to him. That would have solved it. Then he could have kicked Steve's seat, or her mom's. And they would have just smiled and said how cute he was. But she didn't want to sit next to him and listen to him talk about Legos all the way to Boston. She didn't want to sit next to him at all. She didn't want him living in her house half the time and sleeping in what used to be her playroom—she'd had to move everything into her bedroom—and eating the food she had hidden in out-of-the-way places. And, on one particularly awful day, finding her diary that she had hidden in an especially secret spot. Or a spot that she had thought was secret.

"I know this is hard for you, but most kids don't have two bedrooms to themselves," her mom had said, giving Ava a sympathetic look but not backing down. This had been a couple of years ago, back when her mom and Steve got engaged and decided Steve and J.P. would move into Ava's house after the wedding, which had been last year. Not that she had wanted to move into Steve's apartment, or to another house entirely. But what could she do?

"Move in with us," Samantha had suggested. Ava considered it for a few days before concluding that, A) her mom would probably miss her too much, and B) Samantha's parents, who had not been consulted, might not think it was such a good idea. Frequent sleepovers would have to be enough.

Ava was missing school today, which was kind of exciting. The wedding would be tomorrow night, and Sunday there would be a brunch, and then they would fly home Sunday late-afternoon. She couldn't wait for the wedding! There were only two other kids invited besides her and J.P. Their names were Chloe and Nathaniel, and they were the kids of Aunt Suzanne's fiancé's brother. Sort of the equivalent of her, on the other side. Not the equivalent of J.P., as he wasn't a real nephew.

Nor was he a real grandson, but her grandfather, Grandpa Ed, didn't seem to care. He and J.P. got along as if they had known each other forever. Today, after they landed and dropped Ava's mom and Steve off,

Grandpa Ed was planning to take her and J.P. to the house where John and Abigail Adams had lived. Ava had finished a report for school on Abigail Adams a few days earlier, so Grandpa Ed decided this would be a good destination for the three of them while the other adults busied themselves with wedding-related tasks. Ava and Grandpa Ed, a retired history teacher, had always done special history things together. Ava had not been pleased when Grandpa Ed quickly incorporated J.P. into all these excursions. But, again, what could she do?

"Hey, Ava!" J.P. called, kicking her seat and whacking her on the shoulder from behind. "Look! We're over the water!"

"Ow!" Ava cried. "Stop hitting me!"

"Ava," her mom said warningly.

"Well, he hit me!" Why was she blamed for everything?

They were indeed over the water. It was an incredibly clear day, and she could see what looked like a coastline below, and then an expanse of blue. Blue sky, blue water. She decided to pull out her diary and write about it. Ms. Martin, her teacher, had told the afterschool Creative Writing Club, in which she and Samantha were enrolled, that if inspiration struck, to write it down immediately.

Her diary was called Just Putrid, which just happened to be J.P.'s initials. She wrote about all the stupid things J.P. did, and how adults never seemed to be annoyed with him. Samantha's diary was called Samantha Song

Does NOT Like to Sing. This had been Ava's idea. Song was Samantha's last name. "But I do like to sing," Samantha had said, puzzled. "Yes, but that's what's good about the title," Ava had said. "It's ironic."

Ms. Martin had taught them about irony, which meant using words that conveyed the opposite of what someone would expect. Ava thought about it: Wasn't it ironic that Ava, who had been perfectly happy as an only child, now wasn't one any more? Wasn't it ironic that her mother, who seemed perfectly happy in their two-person household, had decided to get married? She had hardly ever even gone out on a date before she met Steve.

Of course, there was a little part of Ava that was happy for her mom. She always felt this tiny twinge of worry about her mom while visiting her dad for most of the summer and during winter break. How was her mom doing? Was she okay? Now Ava's mom had Steve, so when Ava went to California, she felt less worried. But then, J.P. was there at Ava's house part of the time and Ava wasn't, which just made her angry. Why was her mom spending part of the summer with J.P. and not with Ava? Wasn't that ironic?

Ava figured she should write it all in the diary, something her mom encouraged. "Get your feelings out," she often said. "Tell Samantha, tell me, tell Ms. Martin, or just write it in your diary." Ava opened to a new page and started writing. Before she knew it, she felt a bump, and the plane had landed at Logan Airport in Boston.

"Boston!" she heard J.P. saying behind her. "Dad, can we go to the Lego store at the Natick Mall this weekend?" Steve replied something about this being a short trip, and not enough time, and they were going to be busy with the wedding, and J.P. was complaining, and then it was time for them to get their bags out of the overhead bins and leave the plane.

Ava was the first to catch sight of Grandpa Ed waving from inside his dilapidated blue Jeep, which was waiting at the curb when they finally emerged from the terminal. She ran toward him, and Grandpa Ed got out and gave her a huge hug. Naturally, J.P. was right behind her, and Grandpa Ed gave him a big hug too.

They stopped for an early lunch, and then as they settled down for the ride into Cambridge, the adults started discussing the day's plans. J.P., who sat between Ava and her mom, pulled out a few Lego minifigures from his backpack. "See, Ava, this is the young Han Solo," he said, gesturing at one of the figures. "And this is the older Han Solo. I traded with George down the street."

Ava pulled out her book and tried to ignore him. She was rereading all the Harry Potter books for the third time, and was right in the middle of book four. "I've read the first two," J.P. said. "Can I borrow book three from you when we get home? Magic adventures are really cool."

"Mmmph," Ava said, not really paying attention.

"You know when that swirly feeling comes over you and you're about to go back in time or something?" J.P. said.

"Yeah," Ava said, still trying to tune him out. "Swirly feeling, back in time, right."

"I promised Sam I wouldn't say anything, but maybe I can tell you," J.P. said. "I mean, it was amazing!"

Ava was getting annoyed. "I'm trying to read!" she whispered loudly, attempting to keep her voice down and avoid getting her mom involved. "Please!"

J.P. returned to his minifigures and Ava to her book, and soon they pulled into a parking space near Grandpa Ed's apartment. Ava's mom and Steve got out with the luggage. "Have fun with Grandpa Ed, guys," Ava's mom said, and Steve added, "Behave yourselves!" and the two of them headed into the apartment.

Grandpa Ed turned to Ava and J.P. and smiled. "Now off to the John Adams house!"

Ava put her book away. "And Abigail, of course," she said. Having just read several books about the Adams family, she couldn't wait to see where they lived. She had taken a little too long to get started on her project, as often was the case, but once she had plunged into the research, she had found Abigail completely fascinating.

"So, who were they again?" J.P. inquired. "He was a US president, right?"

Ava and her grandfather filled him in on the drive to Quincy. John Adams had been George Washington's vice president, and then was elected the nation's second president in 1796.

"George Washington," J.P. interjected. "Cool guy. You should see him in the middle of a battle!"

Ava shot him a look of scorn. How would he know? Third-graders hadn't even studied Colonial America yet, and J.P. had never seemed especially interested in history.

She turned the discussion back to John Adams as they pulled into a parking lot next to the John Adams Historical Park's visitor center. Adams served one term as president. Abigail Adams, his wife, was perhaps best-known for advising John to "remember the ladies" as he and the other Founding Fathers met to shape their future new country during the Revolutionary War. Their son, John Quincy Adams, later became the sixth president.

The visitor center was filled with books and Adams memorabilia. While Grandpa Ed bought the tickets for the tour, Ava browsed the shelves of books about the Adams family. She had just recognized one that she had read for her report, when she heard J.P. calling. "Ava! Grandpa Ed! Can I get this?"

Ava looked over and saw J.P. holding a box that contained a John Adams bobblehead, one of those figures with the heads that bob up and down. "A John Adams bobblehead?" Ava said, surprised. She had only ever seen bobbleheads of sports figures. "Is there one of Abigail too?" She scanned the shelves, but didn't find one. How unfair and sexist! Of course, there didn't seem to be one of John Quincy either.

"Can I get this?" J.P. asked again, as Grandpa Ed approached. "Look!"

"I don't see why not," Grandpa Ed said. "And for you, Ava?"

Ava chose a copy of the Abigail biography that she had taken out of the library. And the park ranger at the cash register gave Ava and J.P. each a booklet for kids. "If you fill this out, you'll get a prize at the end," he told them.

J.P. opened the bobblehead box as they got on the trolley that was transporting them through Quincy's busy streets to the house where John grew up. Grandpa Ed sat across the aisle, poring over a guidebook.

Ava turned to her booklet and started filling in the answers she already knew: John Quincy Adams was John and Abigail's son. Abigail wrote hundreds of letters to her husband during the many years they were apart. Abigail's daughter, Nabby, short for Abigail, was named for her mother.

J.P. leaned over. "Wow, you've answered a bunch of them already." He flipped through the pages. "This is kind of hard. Maybe it's because they gave me the booklet for age nine and up, and I'm only eight. I guess they thought I looked old for my age." And he smiled proudly. Actually, J.P. didn't look old for his age at all, he looked kind of immature, Ava thought spitefully.

"See? It's John! Hi, John! John, this is Ava," J.P. said, showing the bobblehead to Ava and shaking it a little, so its head bobbed up and down. It was wearing a stern expression. It had receding gray hair, a suit with knickers and a vest, and black shoes with buckles. Ava peered at the bobblehead. It seemed to wink at her, causing her to jump.

"Did you see that?" Ava asked J.P., startled. "It winked!"

"Yeah," J.P. said, smiling happily. "He did wink! Hey, John!"

"Mr. Adams, to you," the bobblehead said creakily, as if it hadn't talked in years. "President Adams, perhaps, but I won't stand on ceremony."

Ava gasped. She started to quiver. She felt as if she must be bobbling more than the bobblehead. What was going on? "It talks!" she managed to say, pointing at it shakily.

"This is so cool," J.P. said, seeming completely unfazed.

"Of course," the bobblehead continued, "I did run into a spot of trouble back in my vice presidential days when I suggested some alternative titles for the presidency. His Elective Majesty. His Mightiness. Naturally, President Washington would have none of it."

Ava remembered reading about that. John Adams had been mocked for coming up with names for the new president that sounded somewhat ridiculous. But what was this? Why was this bobblehead talking? She must be imagining things. Or maybe it was a high-tech bobblehead with some kind of computer chip in it.

"Is the bobblehead really talking?" she asked J.P. "Or am I imagining it?"

"Oh, no, he's definitely talking!" J.P. said. "I don't quite get what he's talking about, but he's talking."

"I think I'm making myself quite clear, young man," the bobblehead said, bobbling his head up and down. "I'm recounting something that happened in my vice presidential days. Not my favorite days, mind you."

"J.P., maybe you should put the bobblehead back in its box now," Grandpa Ed called from across the aisle. He seemed not to have any idea that the bobblehead was engaging in conversation. "You don't want it to break."

"Okay, Grandpa," J.P. said. "Sorry, John, gotta put you away now." And he inserted the bobblehead, grumbling and protesting, back in the box as the bus pulled up at the first stop, a wooden house.

"Break!" the bobblehead was complaining. "I'm not going to break! What is that gentleman thinking?"

A ranger dressed in a tan uniform took the group into the building and J.P. patted the box in an apparent effort to soothe the bobblehead. "This is the John Adams Birthplace," the ranger explained, adding that the building dated to around 1681. The walls were painted white, and some antique-looking wooden furniture was placed around the rooms, which included a parlor and a kitchen.

John Adams Birthplace

As the ranger described the life of the Adams family, J.P. pulled out his booklet and started paging through it. "Hey, what's the answer to this question?" J.P. whispered. "Who wrote the Massachusetts Constitution?"

"Listen to what the ranger's saying," Ava said. "Be quiet!"

Grandpa Ed, who had been focused on the presentation, peered over toward Ava and J.P. questioningly.

"Why, that was I!" came a voice from the bobblehead box. "I wrote the Massachusetts Constitution! I found it most fascinating."

Ava glanced around. The other people on the tour, all adults, seemed not to have noticed the voice. "Shhh," she said, leaning toward the bobblehead box. Was this really happening? Was she talking to a bobblehead?

"I had just returned from serving in France," the bobblehead continued. "It was a challenging assignment, to say the least."

"France!" J.P. exclaimed. "I'm bilingual, you know! I speak French with my mom." That was true. J.P.'s real name was Jean-Pierre, except no one but his mom called him that. J.P.'s mom's family had moved from Vietnam to France many years ago, and she spoke French and English perfectly, and most likely Vietnamese too. Ava was envious. She was looking forward to studying a language next year in middle school. Samantha went to Chinese school and spoke some Chinese, and Sam across the street went to Hebrew school and knew a few words of Hebrew.

"Ah, well, perhaps we can speak French together, young man. I have no doubt your French is better than mine!" the bobblehead exclaimed.

"Ava, J.P.!" Grandpa Ed beckoned to them. The group was exiting the John Adams birthplace and heading to the building next door, the John Quincy Adams birthplace.

"What's going on?" Ava whispered furiously to J.P. as they followed Grandpa Ed into the John Quincy Adams birthplace, which looked a bit larger and had more furnishings. "Why is that bobblehead talking?"

J.P. shrugged. "I don't know," he said. "But this is totally cool! Like I was trying to tell you before, the time with Sam?"

"Sam Adams? My cousin?" the bobblehead said from inside his box. "He was a notable patriot and a well-respected member of our delegation to the Continental Congress. It was he and I and Thomas Cushing and Robert Treat Paine representing our Massachusetts Bay Colony."

"No, not your cousin Sam, our neighbor Sam!" J.P. exclaimed. "Now you're just being silly."

"I, silly? Not likely," snorted the bobblehead. "Although Mrs. Adams sometimes found me so, no doubt."

Ava was having a hard time following this conversation while also trying to listen to the ranger and make sure Grandpa Ed and the other adults didn't hear the bobblehead. How could she possibly explain any of this?

The ranger was saying something that caught Ava's attention, about how Abigail had asked John to send her pins from Philadelphia, as there were few to be had in Boston during wartime. Ava could see J.P. bobbling the bobblehead's head up and down. Suddenly, Ava felt dizzy. She leaned against the yellow-painted parlor wall. The room started spinning, the ranger's voice faded away, and she closed her eyes. When she opened them again, she was still in the room, but the ranger, Grandpa

Ed, J.P., and the rest of the tour group were gone. Instead, she was staring right at a girl about her age who was hovering next to her, looking concerned.

"Where did you come from?" the girl asked. She was wearing a colonial-looking outfit—a long skirt and long-sleeved cotton blouse. Was she some kind of reenactor?

Ava shook her head. "I was right here," she said. "I mean, I was on the tour, and then . . ."

"Tour?" the girl asked. "I don't understand."

Neither did Ava. This must be a crazy dream. She hadn't slept well last night, being excited about the trip and the wedding and all. She still felt dizzy, and she shook her head again to clear it.

"I'm Nabby," the girl said. "Nabby Adams."

Nabby Adams! Abigail's daughter? But . . .

"I'm Ava," Ava managed to say. "Is your mother here?"

"Oh, yes, she's in the middle of writing a letter to our father," Nabby replied. "He's serving in the Continental Congress in Philadelphia. She's telling him about everything we are experiencing here. And she does need some pins. They're awfully hard to come by."

Pins? Like what the ranger had been talking about? Just then, she heard laughter coming from the next room, and suddenly J.P. burst in with three boys—a serious-looking one who appeared to be about J.P.'s age, and two smaller ones. "Hey, Ava, it's John Quincy!" J.P. said, sounding pleased and pointing at the oldest boy. "Plus, here's Charles and Thomas, his brothers! Did they get to be presidents too?"

The children looked puzzled. "Presidents?" John Quincy said. "Presidents of what?"

Of course, they wouldn't know about that yet. This was probably before there even was a president. "Oh, nothing," Ava said, shooting J.P. a warning look. What was he doing here? He was clutching the bobblehead box and smiling, and acting like nothing was out of the ordinary at all.

"Look, guys," J.P. said, opening the box and pulling the bobblehead out. They clustered around, even Thomas, the youngest, who appeared to be no more than three.

"Why, that looks like our father!" Nabby said.

"But older," John Quincy said, reaching out to touch the bobblehead's head, which wobbled and bobbled around for a minute before becoming still.

"Where did you happen upon this toy?" Nabby inquired. "Perhaps we would like one, as we miss Pappa greatly. It would be a comfort to us to have his likeness nearby."

"In the gift shop," J.P. said. "You know, in the visitor center."

The children looked confused. "Your father is indeed famous, and this is a good likeness of him," Ava said, avoiding the question of where the bobblehead came from and trying to speak in a way that would not confuse Nabby and her brothers. "We will try to get one for you."

"Sure!" J.P. said. "I know Grandpa Ed will get us another one!"

Just then, the bobblehead began to quiver and bobble

again, Ava felt her head start to spin, and all at once she was standing next to Grandpa Ed and the ranger. J.P. was there too. Nabby and the boys were nowhere to be seen.

"That was weird," she muttered to herself.

Grandpa Ed and the ranger smiled at her, not seeming to notice anything amiss. "Enjoying the tour?" Grandpa Ed asked. She nodded dumbly.

"Absolutely!" J.P. said. He didn't look dizzy or confused at all. Why not?

"Any questions before you get back on the bus?" the ranger asked.

"Um, how old were the Adams kids around the time Abigail asked John for pins?" Ava asked.

The ranger thought for a moment. "Well, that would have been in 1775, so Nabby would have been about ten, and John Quincy seven or eight, Charles about five, and Thomas, maybe three."

"Okay, thanks," Ava said, feeling a chill run through her. That fit. But had she really met them?

As they trooped outside to board the bus to the next stop, J.P. put the bobblehead, who had fallen silent since the adventure, into its box. "That was so much fun, meeting John Quincy and the others!" he said.

"What is going on?" Ava said. "Don't you think this is weird?"

"Well, I was trying to tell you," J.P. said. "This time travel stuff has happened to me before!"

Chapter

~2~

"What do you mean?" Ava asked as they found seats on the tour bus. She had so many questions. Was her stepbrother some kind of bizarre time-traveling alien? And everyone thought he was so cute. Wait till she told Samantha about this!

Seated once again next to J.P., with Grandpa Ed across the aisle, Ava leaned closer to J.P. so Grandpa Ed couldn't hear. "You've traveled back in time before? Why didn't you tell me? Where did you go? So this really happened? We really met Nabby and John Quincy and the others?" She took a deep breath.

"I tried to tell you," J.P. said. "You know, with Sam?"

"Sam who?" Ava snapped. "What about Sam?"

"Sam from across the street," J.P. said. "He specifically told me not to tell you, but I figured, well, maybe it was okay to tell you, and then this happened, and . . ."

"So where did you and Sam go? When did this happen?" Ava was furious. J.P. had gone off on an exciting time travel adventure with Sam, who after all, was in her fifth-grade class and was someone she'd known practically since infancy? And neither of them had told her a thing?

"Well, you know that hat Sam has? The one he got at Mount Vernon on your class field trip?" Ava nodded. "It's magic! It takes him back to various times in George Washington's life. And one time I got to go along—to some time before the Revolutionary War. George was younger then. He was a British colonel and they were fighting the French. George offered to let me interpret for him, but then the hat came off Sam's head and we ended up back home. Oh, and I left one of my Star Wars ships with George. You know, back in the eighteenth century."

Ava was not only furious, but speechless. Just then, the bus pulled up in front of a large, substantial house set on an expanse of open space. "Peacefield," the driver said, and Grandpa Ed stood up and motioned to them to do the same. "This is where John and Abigail moved after they came back from Europe," Grandpa Ed told them. Looking more closely at Ava, he asked, "Is everything all right?" Ava nodded.

Peacefield

"It's great!" J.P. chirped. Ava shot him a look, hoping he wouldn't say more. She didn't think Grandpa Ed, despite his encyclopedic knowledge of American history, would understand and appreciate the whole time travel thing. She wasn't sure she understood it herself.

Another ranger greeted them and escorted them into Peacefield, which the Adams family bought in 1788. But Ava kept thinking about what J.P. had said.

Oddly enough, it kind of made sense. She thought back to the past week, when her class had performed a play about George Washington. During the rehearsals, Sam had seemed to know an awful lot about George Washington, and kept making what seemed like annoying suggestions about what George Washington might have thought or how George Washington might have moved around. A bunch of kids—herself included, she was now ashamed to admit—had teased him about it. But maybe Sam had been speaking from experience!

So if Sam used a hat to get back to George's time, how did we go back in time? she wondered. Could it have been the bobblehead? But why wasn't it doing anything now? It hadn't said anything for a while. Was it overcome with emotion at seeing its children?

Lost in thought, Ava only partially registered what the ranger was saying. The Adamses added onto the house, Abigail and John both died in the house, and four generations of the family lived there. Eventually it was given to a historical society, which in turn handed it over to the National Park Service.

J.P. was working busily on his guidebook, peppering Grandpa Ed with questions as he wrote down his answers. Ava pulled her guidebook out too. She certainly didn't want J.P. to win some sort of prize while she was left out of the picture.

The ranger took them to the last stop, the Stone Library, filled with thousands of books—approximately 12,000, the ranger said. Ava imagined herself, perhaps with Samantha, or maybe Nabby, reading happily in a corner. But Nabby probably wasn't even alive any more when the Stone Library was built.

When the tour was over and they arrived back at the visitor center, J.P. asked Grandpa Ed if they could get another bobblehead. Was he actually expecting to go back and visit the Adams kids again? Ava wondered. But she had told Nabby and her brothers that she'd try to find one, so she temporarily put aside her feelings toward J.P. and joined in. "Yes, it's not fair that he has one and I don't," she said.

"True enough," Grandpa Ed said, and soon the three of them, plus two bobbleheads and the prizes—special ranger pins—were in the car heading toward Grandpa Ed's apartment.

"Is the rehearsal dinner tonight?" J.P. asked. Ava sighed. Of course it was. Why didn't he remember that? It was at Aunt Suzanne's favorite Chinese restaurant. Chloe and Nathaniel were going to be there, and she had high hopes of getting away from J.P. and hanging out with them. Of course, she had never met them, but they had to be better than J.P. Chloe, she knew, was her age, ten, in fifth grade, and Nathaniel was twelve, in middle school. The same age as Samantha's brother, who, while he generally ignored them, was sometimes in the mood to play soccer with them, or discuss Harry Potter, or something.

Back at the apartment, Ava unpacked and hung her flower girl dress in the guest room closet. She and her mom had always stayed in the guest room together, but ever since her mom and Steve had gotten married, the two of them stayed on the pullout sofa in the living room and she had to share the guest room with J.P. His Legos—how had he managed to fit so many into his backpack?—were already strewn on the floor, and she stepped on one structure and accidentally knocked it over.

"Hey!" J.P. said, running into the room at the sound of the crash. "You broke my Batmobile!"

"Well, don't leave it on the floor, then!" Ava shot back. Maybe she could use Grandpa Ed's phone to check in with Samantha. See how the school day had gone. Tell her about meeting Nabby. But Samantha was probably at soccer practice, since it was late Friday afternoon. Actually, she should call her dad for their daily conversation. She probably wouldn't be able to call him later because of the dinner. She really wished she had her own phone, but her mom and dad agreed that she shouldn't have one until middle school, even though some of her friends had them. All three of the other kids in her class whose parents were divorced had their own phones, Ava had informed her mom. It made it much easier to call the other parent or have them call you. But that argument went nowhere.

As J.P. grumblingly reassembled his Lego, Ava decided to pull out the clarinet she had brought along. Aunt Suzanne and Ava's new Uncle Patrick had wanted Ava and Chloe—who played the flute—to perform a duet at the wedding, and Ava had been practicing for weeks.

She launched into "Sheep May Safely Graze," causing J.P. to shriek and put his hands over his ears. "No, no, not the dreaded clarinet," he moaned, falling backward onto the floor between the twin beds. Ava glared at him but continued to play. Grandpa Ed came in and listened approvingly. He had played the clarinet when he was younger and enjoyed listening to her, Ava knew. She was probably the best clarinet player in the fifth-grade band, if she did say so herself. Samantha played violin in the orchestra and was pretty good too. Ava wondered about Chloe. She and Chloe could probably bond over their musicianship. It would be really nice to have someone to talk to who would be sympathetic. Unlike certain other people she could name.

Ava's mom and Steve were staying at the hotel where the wedding was to take place, along with Aunt Suzanne and Uncle Patrick and some of their guests, and as Grandpa Ed drove Ava and J.P. to the Chinese restaurant for the rehearsal dinner, Ava wondered whether she should say something to her mom about the bizarre meeting with the Adams kids. No, she figured. Her mom would never understand it. She'd probably start analyzing Ava's dreams or something.

The restaurant had a small private room set up for the rehearsal dinner, which really didn't involve any rehearsing. Aunt Suzanne must assume that we all know what to do, Ava thought. It couldn't be that hard to walk down the aisle with Chloe, after all. Spotting her mom standing with Aunt Suzanne, Ava dashed over to give them both big hugs. Aunt Suzanne commented on how tall Ava was getting, and how soon she would leave Aunt Suzanne behind in the height department. "And did you meet Chloe and Nathaniel?" Aunt Suzanne asked. Ava saw two kids with straight white-blond hair sitting in armchairs at the side of the room, engrossed in their phones. "There they are!" Aunt Suzanne said, dragging Ava over to meet them. "Chloe, Nathaniel, this is Ava!" The two of them grunted in response and returned to their phones, and Aunt Suzanne disappeared to talk to someone else.

"Hi," Ava said. Neither of them looked up. "I'm really glad to meet you! Chloe, I know you play the flute, right?" Nothing. They tapped on their screens. This was getting awkward. For the millionth time, she wished she had a phone. Just then, J.P. showed up holding the John Adams bobblehead box. Why had he brought that?

"Hey, guys!" J.P. said. "I'm J.P., Ava's stepbrother." Chloe and Nathaniel grunted again and continued playing a game on their phones. "Look what we got at the John Adams house today!" J.P. continued, and he waved the bobblehead box at them, disrupting their concentration.

"Hey, dude!" Nathaniel said, briefly looking up and frowning. "You just made me mess up this level, and I was about to win! What the heck?" He turned back to his phone, annoyed.

"Yeah, why'd you do that?" Chloe said. But she put her phone down. "What is that, anyway? A bobblehead of John Adams? I have a whole bobblehead collection at home. Mine are a lot better than that. They're mostly of baseball players." She looked more closely at the John Adams bobblehead. "This one's kind of boring."

As Ava glanced over at the bobblehead, she saw that its eyes had narrowed. "What a rude young lady!" it muttered. "No manners!"

Had she heard that, or just imagined it? Ava shot a glance at J.P., who raised his eyebrows. "Oh, wow," Chloe said, revising her opinion of the bobblehead. "I guess it talks. I don't have one like that. What did it say?"

"I couldn't hear it too well," Ava said. No point in

repeating it, although Ava couldn't help agreeing with the bobblehead's assessment of Chloe.

"Do you push a button or something?" Chloe said, grabbing the bobblehead and poking at it. The bobblehead's head started bobbling. Ava felt the swirling feeling come over her again, and suddenly she was in what appeared to be the parlor of the second Adams house, the John Quincy Adams birthplace, with J.P. and Chloe and Nathaniel. Oh, no, what about the rehearsal dinner? What would her mom say? Would they miss the whole thing?

She looked around. Something looked different. And smelled different. There was a fire going in the large fireplace in the parlor.

Chloe and Nathaniel were screaming and clutching their phones, and their pale faces turned even whiter.

"Whoa!" Nathaniel said. "What the heck?"

Chloe let out a whimper. "I feel queasy," she said. "Where are we? Where's the rehearsal dinner? Where are my parents?"

J.P. seemed delighted. "Cool!" he said. "But oh, shoot, we forgot to bring the second bobblehead for the kids!"

"Did you know this would happen?" Ava queried him. She certainly hadn't known, although she had hoped it would.

"No, how would I know?" J.P. said. "I'm not a seer, even though this is my third trip back in time. And only your second. Did you know?"

"Of course not," Ava snapped.

She looked around for Nabby and her brothers, but didn't see any sign of them. Instead, she heard a baby crying and a woman's voice soothing it. And then the woman, carrying a tiny baby, walked into the front room. Ava gasped. The woman had to be Abigail! Or at least, she looked a lot like the painting Ava had seen of her as a young woman. "Hush, Nabby, hush," Abigail said to the baby, who seemed about to fall asleep.

"What is this?" Nathaniel said. "Are we in the middle of a video game or something?"

"Yeah," Chloe chimed in. "There's a cool game where you really feel like you're in some other 3-D world, like the Middle Ages." She gestured at Abigail. "Maybe she's some kind of peasant."

"Peasant!" Abigail said angrily, turning toward Chloe. "How dare you!"

"She's not a peasant, she's Abigail Adams!" Ava jumped in. "And this must be some time around 1765, not the Middle Ages." Ten years earlier than their first visit, since Nabby was a baby.

"Where's John Quincy?" J.P. inquired, looking around the room.

"My grandfather?" Abigail said, looking confused. "He does not live here with us."

"No, John Quincy Adams!" J.P. said. "Your son! I wanted to hang out with him again."

"I have no son," Abigail said. "But this is my baby daughter, Abigail," and she gestured toward the baby, who was now sleeping. "We call her Nabby."

"She's lovely!" Ava said, assuming that mothers always wanted to hear compliments about their babies.

"Why, thank you!" Abigail replied, warming to them slightly. "And who are you? I'm Abigail Adams."

"Yes, we know," Ava said. Nathaniel and Chloe's mouths were hanging open. They seemed to be in a state of shock. "I'm Ava, this is my stepbrother, J.P., and these two are Chloe and Nathaniel."

"Gotta get a picture of this," Nathaniel said, pulling out his phone and tapping at the keys. "What the . . . it doesn't work!"

"Let me try mine," Chloe said. "Maybe we're in the middle of some presidential history app." As the two of them banged frantically on their phones, Ava figured she'd take the opportunity to chat with Abigail. She had read all these books about her, and now here she was!

But before Ava could formulate her first question, Abigail inquired, "And where did you come from?"

"Um, Cambridge," Ava replied. That was where Grandpa Ed's apartment was, and the restaurant too. And it wasn't all that far from Quincy. Saying Bethesda, Maryland, might only prove to be confusing.

"Bethesda, Maryland," J.P. chimed in. "We flew up this morning."

Abigail laughed. "You're a quick-witted one," she said, patting J.P. on the head. "Flew, like a little bird? All the way from Maryland this morning?" She smiled fondly at J.P.

Why did everyone think J.P. was so cute? Even her

own historical idol, Abigail Adams, seemed charmed. The other day, one of Ava's mom's best friends had come over and had given J.P. a big Lego set. And Ava had only gotten two pairs of socks. They were kind of cool, with fun patterns, but they were socks nonetheless. And then Ava's mom's friend had gushed about how cute J.P. was, and how long his eyelashes were. "Wasted on a boy!" Ava's mom's friend had said. Ava had rushed to the mirror to look at her own eyelashes, which were their usual unremarkable selves.

"Hey, Abigail," J.P. said eagerly. "Did you know we have a bobblehead of John? And we got a second one for your kids, except you don't have them yet. Well, except for the baby." He pointed at the sleeping Nabby.

"I'm afraid I don't understand," Abigail said. "A bobbling head of Mr. Adams?"

"You know," J.P. said. "Like what they give out at sports events. A bobblehead." And he started taking the bobblehead out of its box.

"She doesn't know about bobbleheads at sports event!" Ava whispered frantically to J.P. "They don't have those yet either!"

"Oh, right," J.P. said sheepishly. "I guess not."

Meanwhile, Abigail had gone upstairs, perhaps to put Nabby into her cradle. Chloe and Nathaniel were huddled on the other side of the room, deep in an argument.

The front door rattled, and in came a man. He was on the short side and dressed similarly to the bobblehead. John Adams himself! He looked at Ava and J.P. inquiringly.

"Mr. Adams!" Ava said. "What a pleasure to meet you!" J.P. nodded. Chloe and Nathaniel glanced over and came closer when they spotted John.

"We were just visiting Mrs. Adams," Ava continued. "I think she was settling the baby down."

"Yes, yes," John said, sounding somewhat impatient. "Abigail! I have news about the Braintree Instructions!"

Abigail rushed down the stairs. "What, pray tell, has happened?"

"They will be printed in the *Massachusetts Gazette*! Others will learn about our recommendations regarding the Stamp Act!" John said. As Abigail expressed her astonishment, Ava tried to remember what the Stamp Act was. She knew Ms. Martin had mentioned it, and it had come up in some of the books she read for her report on Abigail. She thought it was a tax the British imposed on the colonists before the Revolution.

"What's the Stamp Act?" J.P. asked, breaking Ava's concentration. "Why would you tax a stamp? Is it like, a postage stamp?"

"Why, it's the tax on paper documents that the British Parliament has foisted upon the colonies!" John exclaimed. "As I wrote, it is a most burdensome and likely unconstitutional tax. And the Braintree town meeting has approved the document I wrote in opposition to this tax, and now the document will be published so that more people can see it! The British Parliament, so troublesome!" He shook his head.

"So you don't like British people?" J.P. said, trying to understand. "I know a British person! He lives across the street from us!" Ava sighed. Sam's cousin Nigel, who was in college, did live across the street from them and was indeed from London—she and Samantha loved to listen to him say things in his cool British accent—but that wasn't the point, was it? In fact, at this moment in time, John and Abigail were also technically British, weren't they? There was no United States in 1765.

"Go ahead," Chloe said to Nathaniel, ignoring what John and J.P. were saying and apparently continuing the argument she'd been having with her brother. "Try it."

"Fine," Nathaniel said. He reached out and poked John hard on the arm. "See? He's solid! He's not a ghost!" Chloe looked disappointed.

"What are you doing, young man?" John snapped. "A ghost? Certainly not! What can you be thinking?"

Ava felt she should smooth things over. John, she remembered from her research, had something of a temper.

"I'm sure he didn't think that," she said soothingly.

"I didn't, she did," Nathaniel muttered, pointing at Chloe.

"Did not!" Chloe retorted, and the two of them started arguing again.

"Look, John!" J.P. jumped back into the discussion, waving the bobblehead at John.

"A doll?" John took the bobblehead and looked at it more closely. "Of me? Although I look quite a bit older here. Do I look this elderly, Abigail?"

"Why, no," Abigail said, peering over at it. "This perhaps resembles you in another thirty years' time!"

"See?" J.P. said. "Your head moves up and down and back and forth!" He took the bobblehead from John and Abigail and started moving its head up and down, and then the swirling feeling hit Ava and suddenly she was back in the Chinese restaurant, sitting on the floor next to J.P. She looked up. Chloe and Nathaniel were back in their chairs.

Ava's mom was bustling toward them. "I'm so glad you kids are getting to know each other," she said, smiling. "Have you decided what you'd like to order?"

Were adults just completely clueless about all of this? Ava thought. First Grandpa Ed and the ranger, and now her mom? Hadn't her mom noticed that Ava and the other kids had been absent? Or maybe—weirder still— they hadn't been? Had they been in two places at once?

She really needed to talk to Samantha. "Mom, can I borrow your phone?"

"Not right now," her mom said. "But you do need to call Dad later. We're about to sit down for dinner."

Ava ended up with J.P. on one side and her mom on the other. She had to talk to someone about all of this, and J.P. seemed the only option, unfortunately.

"So were we in two places at once?" Ava whispered to him when her mom began talking to Aunt Suzanne, who was next to her on the other side.

"Huh?" J.P. said, fiddling around with the bobblehead, which was on the table in front of him. "Dang, I really wish you had brought the second bobblehead along. We could have given it to Nabby!"

"How would I know we'd be going back there anyway?" Ava said, glaring at him. "And why would I give a bobblehead to a baby?"

"Yeah," J.P. said thoughtfully. "I guess she'd be a little young to appreciate it. But maybe the next time we visit she'll be older!"

"Do you think there'll be a next time?" Ava asked. She really wanted to talk to Nabby again, and Abigail too. She looked over at the bobblehead, which seemed to nod at her.

Chapter ~3~

Ava put her clarinet together and rummaged through her backpack to find the music for "Sheep May Safely Graze." It was the next morning, the wedding was that night, and Ava's mom had suggested that Ava and Chloe practice their music together. So Chloe and Nathaniel and their parents were on their way over to Grandpa Ed's apartment.

"Where's my music?" Ava asked. Could she have put it somewhere else? Could she have lost it on the plane? She knew most of it by heart, but it helped to have the music there.

J.P. was lying on his stomach, leaning over one of his Lego structures. "Sheep may safely baa," he murmured, moving a Lego mini-figure into its truck. "Cows may safely moo. Horses may safely neigh." And he collapsed into laughter.

"It's a famous piece by Bach! Don't make fun of it," Ava said, annoyed. "Do you know where it is?"

J.P. thought for a minute and reached under his bed. "Is this it?" He pulled out a rumpled set of pages.

"Did you take it?" Ava, furious, grabbed the pages and tried to smooth them out.

"No, it was just right near your diary, and . . ." J.P. clapped his hands over his mouth.

"Were you looking at my diary again?" Ava screamed. Just then, there was a knock on the guest room door and Ava's mom pushed it open.

"Kids, here are Chloe and Nathaniel!" Ava's mom said, a warning look in her eyes as she glanced at Ava.

"He was looking at my diary!" Ava protested, but her mom was already heading back to the living room.

Chloe and Nathaniel pushed their way into the room. "Not much to see in your diary, I bet," Chloe said.

"Burn!" Nathaniel said, making a sizzling noise. He sat down on J.P.'s bed, knocking over one of J.P.'s Legos, which had been perched precariously on the edge, and pulled out his phone.

"Hey!" J.P. said. "Watch out! That was my U-wing fighter!" Nathaniel ignored him. She probably should too, Ava thought. She should ignore all of them. Someone had to be the mature one here. It might as well be her.

She smoothed out the pages of "Sheep May Safely Graze" so they looked almost as good as new, took a deep breath, and turned to Chloe. "Did you bring your music?" Ava's mom had sent Chloe's mom the music. It was arranged as a duet for clarinet and flute, with both parts playing an equal role, and Ava had been practicing her part over and over.

Chloe opened her flute case, quickly assembled the flute, and played a few quick scales. Ava frowned. Chloe sounded pretty good, but her tone wasn't as smooth as that of some of the flute players at Ava's school, Eastview Elementary.

Ava gestured at the music. "So should we start now?"

"Actually, I have some other music," Chloe said. "Here." She removed some music from a folder and thrust it at Ava. Ava looked at it. "But this isn't what we were supposed to be practicing!" The music was centered entirely on the flute, with the clarinet joining in only here and there. "What is this?"

"Sheep May Safely Graze!" Chloe said. "For flute with clarinet."

"Flute with clarinet!" Ava said. "But this was supposed to be an equal duet! That's what my mom sent your mom! That's what I've been practicing!"

"I found this music," Chloe said. "I thought it would work better. I didn't think you would play as well as I do, so I figured this made more sense."

Ava broke her vow to be mature. "I'm the best clarinet player at my school!" she said.

J.P. looked up. "Yeah!" he chimed in, to Ava's surprise. Maybe he felt bad about looking at her diary.

"Why don't you all just shut up?" Nathaniel said

rudely. "I can't focus on this game with all your noise. You can each play a separate song, okay?"

Actually, that kind of made sense. Why should she play a duet with the dreadful Chloe anyway? Just wait till she filled Samantha in on all of this! But what song would she play? They couldn't each play "Sheep May Safely Graze." And would Aunt Suzanne and Uncle Patrick be okay with this last-minute change?

"Fine," Chloe said. "I'll keep 'Sheep May Safely Graze.' I'm sure if you're such a great clarinet player, you'll find something else to play." And she started playing her flute.

"I guess you don't have anything else you can play well enough, then," Ava shot back. She ran through some of the other pieces she knew. She didn't think Darth Vader's march from Star Wars would be appropriate for a wedding.

"That Star Wars march!" J.P. said, eyes gleaming, as if he were reading her mind. "Definitely play that, Ava!" And he started humming it and marching around the small space between the beds, dodging his Legos.

"I don't think so," Ava said. Maybe the "1812 Overture?" She pushed past the others and out to the living room, where the adults were laughing and talking. She wondered how Chloe and Nathaniel could have turned out so horribly when their parents seemed nice enough.

"Ava, sweetheart!" Grandpa Ed gestured Ava over. "I'm going to take you kids on a history walk in a few minutes!"

"Where? And which kids?" J.P. was bad enough, but Chloe and Nathaniel too?

"All four of you!" Grandpa Ed said. "The Freedom Trail! It fits in well with our Adams visit, don't you think?" The Freedom Trail, Ava knew, was a walk through Boston where you could stop at historic sites from the Revolutionary War period. She and Grandpa Ed had been planning to visit it for a while now.

She was excited about the Freedom Trail, but not by the prospect of the three other kids coming along. "Can't we just go together?" she asked. "Just the two of us?"

Grandpa Ed gave her a hug. "One of these days, Ava, we'll do something together, just you and me. But we can't do it today. And I need to get everyone back in time to get ready for the wedding, so we should get started now!"

Amid the flurry of preparations, Ava managed to get Aunt Suzanne's permission to play the "1812 Overture." For someone about to get married, she seemed very relaxed, Ava thought. She thought about her own parents' weddings. Her dad had married Eleanor when Ava was only five, and she could barely remember it. She had been a flower girl then, too. And her mom's wedding had been tiny, just immediate family. Ava had been her mom's maid of honor. Everyone had seemed pretty happy then, too. Maybe she was the only one who felt stressed out.

As Grandpa Ed led them over to the T, the ancient Boston subway system, for the trip to the Freedom Trail, he described the different things they'd see along the trail. The first stop was Boston Common, a huge park-like space that apparently was the oldest public park in the whole country. "They had fireworks here," Grandpa Ed told them. "After the Stamp Act was repealed, and also after the war ended. And bonfires."

"So they did repeal the Stamp Act in the end, then," Ava said, thinking of Abigail and John. "That's good."

She found a pathway leading toward what looked like a gift shop. "See these markings on the pavement? It must be the trail! Can we get something?" she asked

Grandpa Ed.

"Maybe a map," he said. "That might be useful." Following the map, they set out toward the Massachusetts State House, a large imposing red brick structure with a golden dome just up the hill from the Common. J.P. reached into his backpack and pulled out the John Adams bobblehead box. "See, Ava, I brought him along," he whispered. "Just in case. And I brought the second bobblehead to give the kids. I thought you might forget again."

Ava was torn between resentment—was he insulting her?—and feeling oddly grateful that he had remembered to bring both bobbleheads. "Okay, great," she whispered back.

"Oh, you have that bobblehead with you again?" Chloe said, reaching for the box.

"Let go!" J.P. shrieked. "It's my bobblehead!"

"I just wanted to see it!" Chloe said, retreating for the moment. "Is it going to talk again?"

Grandpa Ed, who had persuaded Nathaniel to remove his earbuds and shut off his phone, was explaining something to him about the State House. "Completed in 1798," Grandpa Ed was saying.

J.P. took out the bobblehead. "Hey, John," he said. "We're on the Freedom Trail! Cool, huh?"

The bobblehead blinked a few times. "Please, child, hold me upright so I can see where we are!" J.P. did so, and the bobblehead nodded in a satisfied manner. " Ah, yes, our new State House!" Ava supposed that to

John Adams, a building from 1798 would seem relatively new.

"I heard you discussing the Stamp Act?" the bobblehead asked.

"Yes," Ava said. "I was glad to hear the British got rid of that tax you were so upset about!"

"It only led to more problems," the bobblehead sighed. "That wasn't enough for the British, was it? And then of course there was the Boston Massacre a few years later. You'll be getting to that site soon if we keep walking."

"Hurry up," Nathaniel called back to them. The three picked up the pace.

"Let me hold the bobblehead," Chloe said. "Come on!"

"No," J.P. said.

"Why does it talk?" Chloe asked. "And what happened last night? You know, with the costumes and those people with the baby?"

"It was John and Abigail Adams!" Ava said impatiently. "We told you that already."

"Yeah, right," Chloe said.

Ava shrugged. "Believe what you want to," she said. They had left the State House area and, following the trail, gone down the hill toward a couple of old churches and cemeteries.

"We're short on time," Grandpa Ed said. "I'd love to stop at each one of these sites, but we can't do it today." However, they did stop at King's Chapel and the cemetery adjoining it, which includes the graves of John Winthrop, the first governor of Massachusetts; and William Dawes, who rode with Paul Revere. Around the corner was a statue of Benjamin Franklin.

Suddenly, the bobblehead began grumbling again. "Benjamin Franklin," it muttered. "What problems I had with him. There I was, new to Paris, speaking virtually no French, and did he help me? No!"

"I could have helped you," J.P. said, as they continued down the street. "I speak French."

"Yes, yes, I know, you already told me that!" the bobblehead said impatiently. Ava tried to recall what she knew about John Adams's time in Paris. He had been an envoy there during the war, along with Benjamin Franklin, and it was clear the two of them had not gotten along.

Ava looked up ahead, where Grandpa Ed was again deep in conversation with Nathaniel. Grandpa Ed must have been a really good teacher, she thought, to get Nathaniel interested in history. Nathaniel was pointing at a building they were approaching and seemed to be asking Grandpa Ed a question.

Grandpa Ed stopped and waited for everyone to catch up. "This is the site where the Boston Massacre occurred," he said, gesturing at a corner where a balcony jutted over the street.

"Ah, the Boston Massacre," the bobblehead said, stirring. "That was what I would consider my first really big legal case in my younger days." Ava glanced at

Grandpa Ed, but he didn't seem to notice. Nathaniel, however, looked toward Ava, Chloe, and J.P., who was holding the bobblehead.

"Five colonists were killed here," Grandpa Ed said. "The massacre happened in 1770. A confrontation between several British troops and a group of colonists. And John Adams defended the British troops."

"Aye, that I did," the bobblehead chimed in, nodding its head emphatically. "There were some that said I shouldn't defend them."

"It was an unusual decision," Grandpa Ed continued, unaware of the bobblehead's contribution to the discussion. "Of course, we think of John Adams as a big supporter of the revolutionary cause, not a sympathizer of the Crown. But he most likely wanted to say that justice and the law should come first."

The bobblehead nodded and bobbled some more, agreeing with what Grandpa Ed was saying.

"Was it dangerous for him?" Ava asked Grandpa Ed. "I mean, to support the British soldiers?"

"Aye, the mob was riled up against those soldiers," the bobblehead answered. "I did have some fear for my family, but I thought it was the right thing to do." It paused. "And why are you not addressing me directly, young lady?"

Grandpa Ed, meanwhile, was answering Ava's question, in much the same way as the bobblehead. Ava wasn't sure who to talk to, her grandfather or the bobblehead, and, in an effort not to be rude, she found her head bobbling back and forth between them, and suddenly she felt the swirling feeling and a whiff of cold air, quite different from the warmish late-September breeze, and she was standing in a courtroom, surrounded by yelling people dressed in colonial outfits.

Ava looked around. A group of worn-out men in military uniforms stood in a row—were these the accused British soldiers?—and John Adams, looking angry, was delivering remarks before a crowd of people, mostly men, who were pointing and jeering at the soldiers. She saw no sign of Abigail, Nabby, or the other kids, although if this was 1770, Nabby would only have been about five years old. If Abigail was anything like her own mom, she probably wouldn't have let Nabby come into a courtroom with so many angry people.

She also didn't see J.P., Chloe, Nathaniel, or Grandpa Ed, although she was starting to realize that adults were not part of this time travel experience. They seemed not to notice anything at all. She blinked to clear her head, and suddenly found herself in front of the balcony on the street corner in present-day Boston. The others were still there, discussing the Boston Massacre.

Had she really gone back in time? She jabbed J.P. in the side. "Hey, was I here a minute ago?" she asked him.

"I don't know!" he said. "I was talking with John!" He pointed toward the bobblehead.

No one else seemed to remark on her possible absence, and Grandpa Ed was busy checking his watch. "We should head back pretty soon," he said. "I don't want us to be late for the wedding."

"But we haven't finished the Freedom Trail!" J.P. protested. "We've barely started!"

"We'll have to do it the next time," Grandpa Ed said. "It really does take the entire day, I think."

Chloe and Nathaniel were arguing over a game on Chloe's phone, and Grandpa Ed was busy consulting the map, so Ava leaned toward J.P. "I think I went back to 1770 just now," she whispered. "Just for a minute. I was in a courtroom, and John, I  mean, Mr. Adams, was defending the British soldiers. Everyone seemed very angry."

"They were very angry, young lady," the bobblehead said. "And you can imagine the anger directed at me for defending those British soldiers. But of course I defended them successfully. Most of them were acquitted. One could argue, and I did, that the mob goaded them into shooting."

"Wow," J.P. said. "And why didn't I get to go back with her?" And he looked reproachfully at the bobblehead.

"Next time, we'll go all the way to the Bunker Hill Monument," Grandpa Ed was saying, as they started back to the T stop and the Boston Common. "That's the last stop on the Freedom Trail."

"Ah, Bunker Hill," the bobblehead said, suddenly getting an intense look on its face. "Yes, you must go to Bunker Hill!" All at once Ava felt the swirling again, and she could hear booming sounds in the distance. Two figures loomed by her side. She squinted at them. Was it Abigail and John Quincy? But someone was missing.

She felt a sense of panic, the kind you get when you're having a nightmare and you know something's wrong but you can't quite figure it out. Who was missing? Where was J.P.? But he hadn't been there in the courtroom either and she hadn't felt troubled. In fact, she had felt just fine. Before she could think about it, she was back in twenty-first-century Boston, walking along the sidewalk. She shook herself a little. That was weird. Why had she felt scared?

Ava caught sight of J.P. up ahead chattering with Grandpa Ed. There he was. What had she been worried about? This was all getting too bizarre. She had to talk to Samantha. "Hey, Grandpa, could I borrow your phone?" she asked, running up ahead. "I need to check in with Samantha."

Grandpa Ed handed over the phone, and a minute later, Ava heard Samantha's familiar voice.

"Hermione's fine," Samantha said, sounding excited. "And the soccer game this morning was amazing—I actually scored a goal!"

This was amazing indeed. Neither Ava nor Samantha had ever scored a goal, and they had been on the same soccer team since kindergarten. "Wow, that's incredible!" Ava forgot for a minute about Abigail and John and her weird adventures and listened to Samantha describe her moment of glory. She felt bad that she hadn't been there to witness it.

"I think Hermione was hungry," Samantha said, eventually changing topics. "She seemed really glad to see me. And I saw Sam outside when I was over at your house. He asked where you guys were. It's so funny the way he never listens to anything anyone says! I mean, you told him you were going to the wedding!"

"Yeah," Ava said. Her across-the-street neighbor was incredibly absentminded. Samantha had always kind of liked Sam, but Sam had no clue. And Ava wasn't about to get in the middle of it. She wondered if Samantha's affection for Sam was a result of their having such similar names.

"So how are things going up there?" Samantha inquired.

"Well," Ava began, unsure where to start. Just then, the phone started buzzing. Her mom was calling in, no doubt to inquire where they all were and when they were getting back. "Um, kind of bizarre. But my mom's calling and I need to get off. Talk to you later?"

"OK," Samantha said, and Ava clicked over to her mom. "Ava, honey, where are you?" her mom said, predictably. Ava handed the phone over to Grandpa Ed to explain.

J.P., she noticed, was looking uncharacteristically sad. He was holding up the bobblehead and gently shaking it. "I really, really wanted to go back and see

John Quincy again," he said. "I thought if we were on the Freedom Trail, we might get to go back, you know?"

Ava nodded. "Well, I did get to go back," she said. She wasn't sure if she should mention the second, disturbing, trip to the past. Maybe it had never happened. Maybe it was her imagination. And she wasn't sure why exactly it had been so upsetting.

The five of them packed into a crowded T car and made their way back to Cambridge, at which point there was a rush to get dressed and over to the hotel where the wedding was to be held. As they waited in the hotel lobby, the adults fussed over J.P., who had changed into his tuxedo. Nathaniel was wearing one, too. He snapped a selfie of him and J.P. in their finery. "Dude," he said, giving J.P. a high-five. J.P., who seemed pleased that Nathaniel was actually paying attention to him, smiled as he carefully removed the bobblehead from his backpack.

"Are you bringing the bobblehead to the ceremony?" Ava asked. Her flower-girl dress made her feel grown up. Chloe was wearing a similar dress, but not exactly the same. Aunt Suzanne had said they could each pick something they liked, which Ava appreciated. The idea of wearing exactly the same thing as Chloe, now that she had met her, seemed completely wrong.

"Of course he's coming!" J.P. exclaimed.

The bobblehead nodded and bobbled. "It reminds me of the day I married Mrs. Adams!" it said. "Of course I will attend this wedding!"

Ava sighed. "Okay, but maybe you shouldn't talk during the wedding ceremony."

"Talk!" the bobblehead said angrily. "What do you take me for, young lady? I will allow the happy couple to have their moment!"

"Besides, none of them will notice even if you do talk," J.P. said, gesturing at the adults. "They never do." Ava nodded in agreement.

A photographer appeared and gathered family members into groups. Aunt Suzanne looked beautiful in her wedding dress, which was long and off-white and resembled something from a book Ava had read about flappers from the 1920s.

"I do have a reputation for talking, talking, talking," the bobblehead continued, getting more agitated and nodding and bobbling even more than usual. "But I know when to hold my tongue!"

Ava watched the bobblehead nod and bobble, and then she started feeling dizzy again, and the swirling feeling hit. Her head spun, and she closed her eyes. She heard voices, men arguing, and opened her eyes.

There was J.P., next to her. They were in a room filled with men. Men in wigs seated at wooden desks. She looked around and found John, who looked younger than the bobblehead but older than he had when Nabby was a baby. He was, not surprisingly, in the middle of talking, addressing the group.

"Man, it's hot in here!" J.P. whispered loudly, wiping his brow. He looked sweaty, and so did the men seated around them. Flies buzzed around her head, and she swatted at them.

"Where are we?" she whispered back to J.P.

"How should I know?" he replied loudly. This caused several men to glare in their direction. Ava wondered what they must think, a boy in a tuxedo and a girl in a fancy, twenty-first-century dress. But for the most part, the men ignored them, watching John as he concluded his talk and returned to his seat, which was right next to Ava and J.P.

"Well, hello again," John said. "A pleasure to see you both. As you can tell, we are in the midst of voting on our declaration." Another man got up to speak, and John lowered his voice. "We are finally going to state that we are independent of Britain!"

Ava gasped. "You're voting, right now, on the

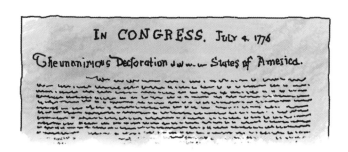

Declaration of Independence?" This was incredible! What a huge moment to be witnessing! J.P. looked excited. Ava glanced around, and was glad that Chloe and Nathaniel were nowhere to be seen. Ha! She could tell Chloe when they got back that she had missed the best part!

"If that's what you'd like to call it, young lady," John said. "I, of course, was instrumental in getting us to this point, although I did encourage Mr. Jefferson to be the one to take the lead role in writing the document. There were five of us on the committee: Mr. Jefferson, Dr. Franklin, Mr. Livingston, Mr. Sherman, and myself."

"You mean, Thomas Jefferson and Benjamin Franklin?" Ava interrupted. "And is this a meeting of the Continental Congress? In Philadelphia?" She remembered some of this from Ms. Martin's class.

"Why, of course, young lady, of course!" John said impatiently, mopping his brow. "I told Mr. Jefferson that he, as a Virginian, should take the lead. I furthermore told him that I am far more obnoxious and unpopular than he, and thus unsuited to the task, and I concluded by informing him that his writing was far superior to mine."

"Is that true?" Ava asked, feeling some loyalty to John. "I thought you were a good writer."

"Why, thank you, young lady. I admit to having quite the felicitous pen at times, but I think it worked out quite well to have Mr. Jefferson write the document."

"Yeah, I guess it did," Ava said, astounded by this conversation.

"Hey, John," J.P. burst into the discussion. "I brought the bobblehead again!" As he removed it from his backpack, several sweaty gentlemen leaned over to take a look.

"Why, it quite resembles Mr. Adams!" one of them said.

"It is I," John said proudly. "Although I admit it does look older than I do."

Just then, Ava had a terrible thought. The wedding was about to start! And she and J.P. were not at the hotel, they were in Philadelphia in July 1776. And as exciting as that was, she needed to get herself—and J.P.—back to twenty-first-century Cambridge, Massachusetts. Her mom would be very upset, as would Aunt Suzanne and Grandpa Ed. And Chloe would have the musical spotlight entirely to herself.

Ava grabbed for the bobblehead. "Hey!" J.P. said. "Let go!" But Ava didn't; she gave the bobblehead a little shake.

"We need to get home," she said. "I mean, the hotel, back in twenty-first-century Cambridge! Please!"

The bobblehead nodded and bobbled and winked, and a minute later Ava found herself next to J.P., on a sofa in the hotel lobby. Chloe was standing over them, smirking.

"I guess you guys missed the photos!" she said, sounding quite pleased. "We were looking everywhere for you! Everyone was really mad!"

"I guess you missed the vote on the Declaration of Independence," Ava retorted. "Back in 1776. Oh well, too bad!"

"Yeah!" J.P. chimed in. "It was really cool!"

"Here you are!" Ava's mom and Steve rushed over to them. "We've been looking all over for you! We need to take some photos right now!"

Ava looked over her shoulder at Chloe as she, J.P., her mom, and Steve headed to a corner of the room with the photographer. Chloe was standing beside Nathaniel, and the two of them looked annoyed. Good!

Chapter ~4~

va walked down the aisle behind Aunt Suzanne and Grandpa Ed as a trio of musicians played the "Wedding March." She remembered her mom's instructions to walk slowly, hold her bouquet upright, and stand up straight. Next to her, unfortunately, was Chloe, but Ava tried to ignore her.

Which was difficult. Chloe was walking slowly too, and kept smiling at the people on either side of the aisle and tossing her hair around. As if she were the bride, Ava thought. Not that Aunt Suzanne was tossing her hair around or anything.

Reaching the end of the aisle at last, Ava took her place next to J.P., who held a small velvet case with the rings. He had been persuaded to leave the bobblehead in its box on a chair in the front row, but he kept casting worried glances at it.

"I'm nervous that he feels left out," J.P. whispered to Ava. "He told me he wants to come out of the box and see the wedding."

"Well, he can't!" Ava whispered back. "Shhh! It's

almost time for you to give them the rings!" Just then, everyone turned, beaming, toward J.P.

He presented the rings with a flourish, and some of the wedding guests laughed. Ava could hear one lady saying, "Oh, how cute!" Of course. Ava had received compliments on her dress. But it wasn't the same.

After Aunt Suzanne and Uncle Patrick were pronounced a married couple, Chloe began to play "Sheep May Safely Graze." Ava found herself playing an imaginary clarinet, her fingers going over the song she had practiced so many times. She felt a flash of annoyance as the song came to an end and an appreciative murmur floated through the audience. Chloe bowed and smiled, nodding back and forth to all corners of the room. All that nodding reminded Ava of the bobblehead. She pictured Chloe as a bobblehead. Maybe it could be given out as a prize for the Most Annoying Cousin-in-Law Contest, or whatever relation Chloe was to her now. She wished she had Just Putrid so she could write this down.

J.P. was nudging her. "Get your clarinet!"

Ava startled. The wedding party had started processing back down the aisle, her cue to play the "1812 Overture." She found the clarinet and started to play, but everyone's attention was on Aunt Suzanne and Uncle Patrick. She wished she could have played during the ceremony. Like Chloe.

"That was beautiful, Ava!" her mom said. Everyone was milling around, waiting to go into another room for dinner. Waiters were circulating with drinks and hors d'oeuvres.

"Thanks," Ava said. She caught sight of J.P., who had pulled the bobblehead out of its box and seemed to be arguing with it.

"I know you wanted to see it, but everyone told me you had to stay in the box!" J.P. was saying as Ava approached. "You know, safely out of the way!"

The bobblehead sputtered angrily. "Stay in a box!" it exclaimed. "Well, really! As I told you, I am perfectly capable of remaining silent when necessary!"

Ava joined in. "Well, now you're out," she said. "See? Look how pretty Aunt Suzanne's dress is."

"Ah yes," the bobblehead said. "Lovely. Mrs. Adams looked beautiful at our wedding, too." A dreamy expression settled over its features.

Chloe and Nathaniel joined them just as a waiter came by with a tray of appetizers. J.P. helped himself to two small egg rolls. "Egg roll?" he said, offering one to the bobblehead.

"A roll of egg?" the bobblehead said, looking confused. "I'm not familiar with that. Some newfangled concoction, no doubt?" It paused. "I did encounter many new foods in my travels, but a roll of egg was not among them."

"It can't eat egg rolls," Chloe said scornfully. "What are you thinking?"

"Why, certainly I could eat them," the bobblehead said. "If I wanted to, that is."

"But you're a bobblehead," said Nathaniel.

"What do you eat, anyway?" J.P. inquired.

"I always enjoy good New England fare," the bobblehead

replied. "Of course, while representing America in Europe, as I mentioned, I did need to broaden my palate somewhat."

"Where did you go besides France?" Ava asked, trying to remember.

"Oh, Holland. And back to France again," the bobblehead said, waving one hand around. "What a pleasure it was when Mrs. Adams could join me at last. And Mr. Jefferson was there too, of course. And eventually I found myself representing America in London." The bobblehead started nodding and bobbling, and Ava found herself nodding and bobbling back at it, and then the dizzy feeling hit and she was . . . where?

She gazed around. Back in the John Quincy Adams birthplace. As were J.P., Chloe, and Nathaniel. But what year was it this time? She heard a clattering at the front door and suddenly Nabby burst in, followed by her brothers. They seemed to be about the same age as when Ava had met them the first time. Maybe a bit older.

"Oh, hello!" Nabby said, sweaty and out of breath but not surprised to see Ava and the others. "We were outside doing some chores, but Charley and Tommy were quarreling so we came back in."

"Mamma!" Charles bellowed. "Where are you?"

Abigail hurried down the stairs. "Oh, children! I thought you were out taking care of the chores! With your father away so much, it's important that we keep up with . . ." She broke off, noticing that there were twice as many children in the room. "Why, it's you again," she said, a mixture of curiosity and annoyance on her face.

"Yes, we came for a quick visit," Ava improvised. "We don't mean to interrupt."

"No, no," Abigail said. "It's undoubtedly a good idea for the children to have friends to spend time with. Things have been difficult," she added, sighing. "Such privations with the war going on, and it's quite a burden with Mr. Adams in Philadelphia."

"Yeah, he was really busy writing the Declaration of Independence when we saw him!" J.P. exclaimed. Ava groaned. Why didn't he ever seem to understand what would be confusing for the Adams family? Maybe this was before the Declaration of Independence had even been thought of!

"What's the Declaration of Independence?" John Quincy asked, his serious face puzzled. "When did you see Pappa? And how do you know what he is doing, anyway?"

"Be you spies?" Abigail asked warily.

"No, of course not!" Ava said. "My stepbrother was just using his imagination!" She gave J.P. a poke in the side.

"Ow!" J.P. exclaimed. "What was that for?"

"Did you bring the toy that resembles Father?" Nabby asked. "The one you spoke of last year?" Aha, Ava thought. So it was 1776, but they didn't know about the Declaration of Independence yet. It seemed to be summertime, given how hot everyone looked. It was certainly warm in the house.

"Dang!" J.P. exclaimed, pulling the bobblehead out. "We have this one, and we were going to bring the second one to give you, but we were coming from the wedding, and things were really crazy when we were getting ready, and . . ."

"Which wedding?" Nabby inquired, reaching for the bobblehead, which J.P. handed over. "How romantic!"

"Oh, it was beautiful," Ava said. "My aunt. Their uncle," and she gestured toward Chloe and Nathaniel, who, once again, were unsuccessfully attempting to take photos of the Adams family with their phones.

"I played a lovely flute solo," boasted Chloe.

"Well, I have tasks to accomplish," Abigail said, not seeming to care about Chloe's flute prowess. "A pleasure to see you again." And she headed back upstairs. At least she seemed reassured that they weren't spies, Ava thought. It would be awful to have your historical idol think ill of you.

"What did the bride wear?" Nabby asked eagerly. "I've often wondered about my own wedding one day. Perhaps I'll marry a soldier."

Ava described Aunt Suzanne's dress, while trying to remember if Nabby had actually ended up marrying a soldier. She thought she had, but she wasn't sure.

"It sounds wonderful," Nabby sighed. "I imagine I'll have a lovely gown, and my husband will be quite handsome. Do you wonder sometimes about that, Ava?

About your wedding?"

Ava always supposed she'd get married one day, but she had never imagined the ceremony. It would be nice if it could be outdoors, she thought. Maybe in a garden. "Well," she began.

"I'll have a really expensive designer wedding dress," Chloe proclaimed. "Maybe I'll have one of those destination weddings. Like in the Bahamas or Mexico or somewhere like that. My friend's cousin did that."

"The Bahamas? Mexico?" Nabby looked puzzled.

Charles, bored with the wedding talk, leaned forward. "We're going to be inoculated soon!" he confided. "From smallpox! The pox is everywhere!"

Ava hadn't thought of that. Oh, no! Could she and J.P. and Chloe and Nathaniel get smallpox from being here? Were they immune? And what exactly was smallpox, anyway?

"Smallpox!" Chloe said. "Ew! Get me out of here!"

"We are to travel to Boston," Nabby said, gently bobbling the bobblehead's head. "Mamma and the four of us are to be inoculated there."

"We could die," John Quincy said, looking grave as he reached out and patted the bobblehead. "The inoculation itself carries great risk. But Mamma says 'tis better to take that risk than to do nothing."

Ava tried to remember what she had read about this for her Abigail Adams report. It had been the summer of 1776. Smallpox was definitely a problem, and Abigail had decided to take the four children to Boston to be

vaccinated. At least one of them had become very sick—
Nabby, she thought—but they all survived. Abigail's
husband John, away in Philadelphia, had only learned
about the inoculations after the fact.

"You will survive," Ava said. "I just know it."

"I hope you are right," John Quincy said, his brow
furrowed.

"I read something about that type of inoculation,"
Nathaniel said. "It wasn't just like getting a regular shot,
I mean, like we would get. It was a lot more risky."

"What is a regular shot?" Nabby asked, bobbling the
bobblehead's head some more before handing it back
to J.P.

"Um," Nathaniel said. "Well, like, just with a needle
and all?"

J.P. began vigorously bouncing the bobblehead up and down. "I hate shots!" he said. Ava nodded in agreement, and the bobblehead kept nodding and bobbling, and then the swirling feeling came and the Adams kids weren't there any more, and Ava and the others were back in the hotel, and a waiter was standing in front of them with a tray of glasses. "Champagne?" he said. "But apple juice for all of you! Parents' orders." And he winked.

"Champagne?" the bobblehead asked. "From France, no doubt."

"*Mais oui*," J.P. replied. "But of course!"

As Ava sipped her apple juice, her mom approached, holding out her phone. "It's Dad," she said

Ava took the phone and retreated into a corner. "Hey, Dad," she said.

"Ava!" her dad said. "Eleanor and I are going to the theater later, so I wanted to catch you now. How was the wedding?"

"We're still there," Ava said. "The dinner's about to start." She could envision the house in California, the living room where he was probably sitting now, a couple of the dogs on the sofa with him. She was definitely a cat person at her mom's, but at her dad's she became a dog person. She loved to take them out for walks around the neighborhood.

"Your mom said you went on the Freedom Trail today with Grandpa Ed—how did that go?" her dad asked. Should she tell him? Probably not. She didn't think he would understand her new friendship with the Adams family.

"Great!" she said. "It almost seemed as if the characters were coming to life!" That was an understatement, for sure.

"Wonderful," her dad said. "Ed's always been good at bringing history to life. Really an amazing teacher! So I ran into Hailey and her mom at the supermarket today. She asked when you'd be out here again, and I told her December."

Ava smiled thinking of her best California friend. Certainly no substitute for Samantha, but a good friend nonetheless. They went to day camp every summer and hung out at each other's houses. "Tell her hi from me," Ava said. Samantha had, at various points, expressed curiosity about Hailey, and the three of them had spoken on the phone a few times. It had felt a little weird. Sort of as if Ava had a split personality.

"What's it like?" Samantha had asked recently. "Going off to California for all those vacations and having, like, this whole different life out there?"

Ava hadn't known what to say. It was how her life had always been. Her parents split up when she was three, and soon after, her dad moved to California to join his brother's veterinary practice. She couldn't even remember when they were married. Ava's paternal grandparents lived in California too, and she got to spend a lot of time with them during her vacations. "Okay, I guess," she had told Samantha. "I mean, it's just what I'm used to."

Ava seemed to be the only one in her class who traveled such a long distance between parents. The divorced parents of the other kids lived nearby, and the kids spent time with both of them during the week. Then there was J.P., who spent half his time at her house and half his time with his mom and stepdad. She wished he would spend most of his time at his mom's, but then Steve would probably miss him.

Suddenly she realized she hadn't heard what her dad was saying, something about a cat he had treated recently. "Pretty funny, huh?" he concluded.

"Yeah," Ava said.

"Is everything okay?" her dad asked. "You seem a little . . . I don't know, tired, maybe?"

"I'm not tired!" she said. She wasn't a toddler, she was ten.

"Well, I'll let you get back to the wedding, sweetheart. Lots of love, and from Eleanor too." They said their good-byes and Ava returned the phone to her mom.

"Good talk?" her mom asked. Ava nodded. "We're about to go in to dinner now," she continued. "There's a special table for you and the other kids."

Was she supposed to be happy about being seated with J.P., Chloe, and Nathaniel? There was nothing special about that, as far as she was concerned. "Can't I sit with you and Grandpa Ed?" she said, realizing she sounded whiny.

"Your table is right near ours," her mom replied.

"You can come over whenever you want."

Ava sighed. Entering the room, she saw that J.P., Chloe, and Nathaniel were already seated. Chloe and Nathaniel were, of course, playing games on their phones, and J.P. was pulling the bobblehead out of its box. Reluctantly, she sat down.

"Paris," the bobblehead was saying. "Auteuil, to be exact. A beautiful home. Enormous, really. And the gardens were something to behold."

"My grandparents live in Paris," J.P. said. "Maybe the next time I visit I can see where you and Abigail lived!"

"Maybe sooner!" the bobblehead said with a gleam in its eye. It started nodding and bobbling in excitement. Ava tried not to look at it. She didn't think they should be going anywhere in the middle of the wedding dinner. Maybe Aunt Suzanne would want Ava to make a speech or something. But she couldn't look away. And as the swirling feeling hit, she gave in to the inevitable.

She opened her eyes to find herself standing in a garden. A house—the biggest house she'd ever seen!—loomed beside her. And the gardens stretched out for what seemed like miles.

"Whoa!" said J.P., who appeared next to her. "It's a total mansion! I want to live there! Do you think we can go in?"

"Maybe," Ava said. She wouldn't mind taking a look herself. But then she heard voices coming from around the corner. A group of people strolled into view, and she pulled J.P. behind a convenient shrub. She recognized John, and then Abigail, and two people who looked like teenagers, and then a tall man with reddish hair. A couple of other men trailed behind them. Servants?

"Shall we sit?" Abigail said, gesturing to a small table set with fine china and various delicacies. "Mr. Jefferson?" she beckoned to the tall man. Thomas Jefferson! The bobblehead had mentioned that they'd been in Paris together.

"Why, thank you!" Thomas Jefferson said, sitting down next to Abigail. Ava squinted at Thomas Jefferson. Or not at him, but at something behind him. It was shiny and bright.

"Do you see something?" she said, nudging J.P. "Right behind Thomas Jefferson?"

"Which one's Thomas Jefferson?" J.P. said, peering over the bush.

"The tall one with red hair next to Abigail."

"Wow, Abigail and John look older, don't they!" J.P. said. "And who are those teenagers?"

"Maybe Nabby and John Quincy?" Ava said. How fascinating! They looked completely different. She wondered if they would remember her and J.P.

"I mean that thing sort of glowing, behind Thomas Jefferson."

"Oh, yeah," J.P. said. "What is it? I want to go investigate!" He came out from behind the bush and ran toward the table. Ava followed. The party around the table, all seated by now—except for the two additional men, who hovered nearby—turned to look at the two of them.

Nabby, for it was indeed Nabby, was the first to recognize them. "It's Ava and J.P.!" she said. "My goodness, it's been so long!"

"Hello, Nabby, John Quincy, Mr. and Mrs. Adams, Mr. Jefferson," Ava said, nodding, bobblehead-like, at all of them. "It's great to see you again!" She wondered how they remembered her. If Nabby and John Quincy were teenagers—and they looked like older teenagers rather than younger ones—it must be well into the 1780s by now. And what did she and J.P. look like? Did they look like teenagers too? She wished she had a mirror!

"Bonjour!" J.P. said, and rattled off a quick stream of French. The others seemed to understand, because they smiled and said, "Charming!" Of course.

"And you still have the toy that resembles Father," John Quincy said, looking at the bobblehead.

J.P. smacked his forehead. "Yes, and we keep forgetting to bring you the second one." Although maybe they were too old for it now, Ava thought.

"Please, join us," Abigail said. "We are still accustoming ourselves to this extremely large house and all the servants! And this wonderful lawn!"

Ava and J.P. sat down and helped themselves to the bread and pastries. They were scrumptious. Here she was, in France, eating real French pastries! It was her first time out of the United States, and she had traveled here without a passport! Amazing! Samantha would be so jealous. Not to mention Chloe.

"Mr. Jefferson was just telling us of some of his latest purchases," Abigail said.

"Yes, new fancy French clothes, wine, even a new sword," John added. Ava looked at Thomas Jefferson, still puzzled by the shining thing behind him. Thomas Jefferson's clothes were fancier than those of the Adams family, although they were dressed more formally than they had been in Boston.

Thomas Jefferson smiled faintly and nodded. "All true," he said. "And more books, too."

"So can I see it?" J.P. asked.

"See what?" Thomas Jefferson replied, seeming puzzled.

"The sword!" J.P. said. "Obviously!"

"Ah, well, the sword is only for use with certain clothes," Thomas Jefferson said. "But perhaps you can see it another time. We could make use of you as an interpreter, perhaps, eh?" He turned to John.

"Excellent, yes," John said. "My French has greatly improved, but I do not know that I would describe myself as completely fluent."

"And I certainly am not," Thomas Jefferson said.

"I am," J.P. chirped. "I'm bilingual!" Ava could have sworn J.P. had told John that already, but maybe it was the bobblehead he had told. It was confusing.

"We shall have to take you on as our young interpreter, then" John said, ruffling J.P.'s hair as Abigail smiled down at him. Ava rolled her eyes.

"George wanted to use me as an interpreter, too," J.P. continued. "George Washington. It was during some war or other. With the French. But it didn't work out."

"What a lively imagination," Abigail said fondly.

Meanwhile, the shining form had moved from Thomas Jefferson's side and was approaching Ava. It seemed to be waving at her, trying to get her attention. What on earth was it? This time travel thing was getting stranger and stranger. The form was coming closer, and somehow it made her think of Ms. Martin's classroom.

J.P., next to her, was showing the bobblehead to Thomas Jefferson, who was across the table from him. "It's John!" J.P. exclaimed. "See?"

"Extraordinary!" Thomas Jefferson said, taking the bobblehead and examining it closely. "Where did you come by this toy?"

"The John Adams Visitor Center," J.P. said.

"You have a center for visitors?" Thomas Jefferson said, raising an eyebrow at John, who smiled in an unusually modest way.

"I suppose I do," John said, looking pleased.

Just then, the bobblehead, delighted to be the center of attention, started nodding and bobbling. The glowing blob was beside her now, waving its arms, and Ava felt dizzy.

And then she was back at the table in the Boston hotel with J.P. and the bobblehead. A waiter leaned over. "Do you want your salad?" he asked. "Or should I take it away?"

va had just finished the main pasta course when the music got louder and people started heading for the dance floor. Her mother and Steve joined them and began to dance in that awkward parental way. She felt embarrassed for them. J.P. nudged her, pointed at them, and giggled. The bobblehead perked up and looked over at the dancers.

"What sort of music is this?" it asked, curious. "It's so loud! I've never heard anything like it! In France, I came across various things I had never heard before, but this is quite the novelty!" And it started bobbling and nodding in time to the music. Ava watched it, but it didn't seem inclined to go on any time travel adventures. "Why, I'm finding this most enjoyable," it said.

"Look, it's dancing!" Chloe said, staring at the bobblehead. "Nathaniel! Look!"

Nathaniel glanced over. "Cool," he said. "Boogie down, John!"

Grandpa Ed chose that moment to amble over. "Not much of a dancer, myself," he shouted over the music, as he pulled up a chair. Ava wondered if he'd say something about the boogie-ing bobblehead, but, once again, he didn't notice. "Enjoying yourselves?" he asked, looking around at the four of them.

They nodded.

"I see you've brought the bobblehead," Grandpa Ed shouted toward J.P.

J.P. laughed. "See, he's dancing, Grandpa! He's enjoying the music!"

Grandpa Ed laughed. "Of course he is," he said loudly, with that "you're so cute" look that adults always got around J.P. "It's too bad we didn't find an Abigail bobblehead so they could dance together!"

Ava considered whether Grandpa Ed had ever enjoyed dancing. Maybe when her grandmother was alive. She had died before Ava was born. Ava knew Grandpa Ed had had various girlfriends, or "lady friends" as he called them, but he hadn't brought anyone to the wedding, so she assumed there was no one in the picture now. She and Samantha had thought about fixing up Grandpa Ed with one of the teachers at Eastview. She was divorced and kind of old and seemed really into history.

"Hey, Grandpa," Ava said, remembering the conversation. "Do you want to meet this really nice teacher at my school?"

Just then, the music reached a crescendo and the bobblehead executed an amazing dance move, pirouetting around the table and knocking over Chloe's water glass.

"Dang!" Chloe said, mopping up the water with her

napkin. "What the heck?"

J.P. and Nathaniel were snickering, and Ava couldn't help stifling a laugh. "Great moves, John!" J.P. exclaimed, rescuing the bobblehead from the water.

Grandpa Ed, who had missed the whole thing, turned toward Ava. "Sorry, Ava, dear, I couldn't hear you. What did you say?"

The bobblehead began to splutter and shake off the drops of water. "Brrrrr," it said, and shivered. "Ice water! Colder than a New England pond! Please, someone wipe me off with some nice dry linens!"

Ava gathered the bobblehead in her napkin and carefully dried it. "Sorry, Grandpa, we can talk about it later," she shouted. It was too loud to have a conversation anyway.

The waiter came by with slices of cake, and Grandpa Ed headed off to his own table.

"Cake?" J.P. asked the bobblehead, his mouth full of cake.

"Oh, here we go again," Nathaniel said. "It's a bobblehead! It doesn't eat!"

"Ah, but I do eat!" the bobblehead said, bobbling indignantly. "I am perfectly able to eat! It's a question of wanting to do so." As it continued to bobble up and down, Ava's head started spinning. Then she closed her eyes and heard a loud noise, like the sound of hundreds of people cheering.

When she opened her eyes, she was standing on a balcony. Below were, indeed, hundreds, if not thousands, of people in eighteenth-century garb. They seemed very excited. What are they so excited about? Ava wondered. Certainly not to see her.

Some of the people waved at her, and she ventured a smile in return. She felt like a princess, standing on a balcony like this with adoring crowds below. Like the royal family on the balcony at Buckingham Palace in London, perhaps. But of course, that went against the whole idea of the American Revolution. "Where is President Washington?" a woman called up to her. President Washington? Ava had no idea!

"I'm sorry, I don't know . . ." she began, when J.P. appeared next to her. "He's inside!" he interrupted. "He'll be out soon!" He waved to the crowd, and people waved back happily.

Ava turned to him. "How do you know where he is?" she said, feeling her usual impatience.

"I saw him!" J.P. said, continuing to wave. "He was surrounded by a group of people, so I couldn't say hi. You know, I'm sure George remembers me from that other time."

Ava wondered about that, but she was curious. Was George Washington really inside, presumably in a room off this balcony? And what year was this anyway?

She turned and headed into the large, ornate room, with J.P. following. And there, towering over the others, was George Washington himself, dressed in a brown suit. Next to him was John Adams, who spotted her and strolled over.

"Excellent, excellent," John said, rubbing his hands together. "The inauguration of our first president, and you are here to see it! What a historic moment for our country!"

"What is today's date?" Ava asked, unable to remember when George Washington was inaugurated.

"Why, April the 30th, in the year 1789," John replied, surprised at her ignorance. Out of the corner of her eye, she noticed that J.P. had reacquainted himself with George Washington, who was smiling fondly as he leaned down to speak with him. George Washington, too? Ava thought. How frustrating! Did every famous historical figure have to think J.P. was cute?

"And where are we?" Ava asked.

"New York City!" John said, his surprise deepening. "Our nation's capital! Where else would we be?"

"Of course," Ava said, having forgotten that New York was once the capital of the United States. Hoping to redeem herself, she added, "And you also are to be inaugurated today as vice president?"

"Of course not, child!" John said impatiently. "I was sworn in as vice president nine days ago!"

"Oh," Ava said, puzzled. Weren't presidents and vice presidents sworn in on the same day? At least, in modern times?

George Washington strode over, with J.P. galloping behind. "So you are J.P.'s stepsister?" he inquired, offering his hand to Ava. "A pleasure to meet you!"

"Thank you, sir," Ava managed to reply. "I mean, Mr.

President. An honor to meet you!" Wow, George Washington himself!

"And Vice President Adams!" George Washington said, putting his hand on John's shoulder. "Excuse me, children, I must steal him away."

The men headed for the balcony. Ava and J.P. followed, trying to see what was going on. The roar of the crowd got louder. A government official handed George Washington a Bible, and George Washington began taking the oath of office, repeating the words after the other man. Ava watched, holding her breath. Samantha wouldn't believe any of this! Ava needed to write it all down in Just Putrid as soon as they got back.

"Long live George Washington, President of the United States," the man called out. The crowd burst into applause and cannons began firing.

As George Washington, John, and the others turned to go back into the room, J.P. darted between two men onto the balcony, and the crowd started cheering for him. He bowed and waved the bobblehead at the crowd.

"Stop it!" Ava cried, yanking his sleeve. "What are you doing?" Really, he was so annoying! This was so inappropriate! He had no respect for history!

"Why should I?" J.P. said, not stopping at all.

Ava gave up and went inside. George Washington, who, oddly, looked a little nervous, was preparing to make a speech. His inaugural address? J.P. should get back in to hear this, she thought.

"Fellow Citizens of the Senate and the House of

Representatives," George Washington began. "Among the vicissitudes incident to life, no event could have filled me. . ." Ava spotted J.P. coming toward her.

"I think this is his inaugural address!" Ava whispered. "You should stay here and listen!" John beckoned the two of them to stand near him. As she listened to the speech, Ava scanned the room to see if she could find any other famous people. But a smaller figure caught her eye. He was about her size and had slipped in next to a couple of the men. She peered over. Was that Sam? Her across-the-street neighbor?

"Oh, man, Ava!" J.P. said in a voice too loud to be a whisper, earning a frown of disapproval from John. "It's Sam!" He pointed across the room at their neighbor.

What on earth was Sam doing here? From what J.P. had told her, Sam's hat took him back in time. And he was indeed wearing his hat.

"This must be another place the hat took him!" J.P. said, whispering quietly now. "You know, like the time I went with him!"

Ava was still in a state of disbelief. Were there other time-traveling kids they might run into? People they knew? Maybe everyone had a magic thing—hat, bobblehead, something else—that took them back in time. Maybe Samantha did, and just hadn't told her.

". . . and the wise measures on which the success of this government must depend," George Washington said. He took a deep breath and stopped speaking. At once, everyone in the room started talking, and many people made their way over to the new president to offer congratulations.

"Come!" John said to Ava and J.P. "Let us wish our new president well!" The three of them moved closer to George Washington, who was already surrounded by well-wishers. Suddenly, Ava spotted Sam a few feet away.

"Hey, there he is!" J.P. shouted over the hubbub. "Hey, Sam! Sam!" The two of them made their way over to their neighbor, but he didn't seem to see them. Instead, he kept squinting in their direction and blinking.

"Sam!" she shouted, reaching out and touching his arm. "What are you doing here?" There was no response.

"I don't think he can see us," Ava called to J.P.

"Why not?" J.P. replied. "Sam! Hey, Sam! It's us!"

It was as if they were invisible, except that he kept blinking and squinting whenever he looked in their direction.

"Come on," Ava said, disappointed, pulling J.P. back toward John. "He can't hear us, either!"

"Sam!" J.P. called once more, before shrugging and giving in. Ava noticed that Sam was talking to George Washington, who seemed delighted to see him. In fact, they were having a long, animated conversation. Just then, several others joined them, and one of them took off his hat politely as George Washington introduced them to Sam. Sam did the same—and suddenly disappeared.

"What?" Ava said, shocked. "Where did he go?"

"That's what happens with the hat," J.P. said, unruffled. "Once he takes it off, he ends up back in the twenty-first century. He shouldn't have taken it off!" He shook his head disapprovingly.

By then, the three of them had reached George Washington and offered their congratulations.

"Oh, George," J.P. said excitedly. "I almost forgot to show you my John Adams bobblehead! I want to get one of you, too!" He pulled out the bobblehead.

"How fascinating!" George Washington said. "I still have that Star Wars ship you gave me all those years ago!" Ava wondered again how these historical figures seemed not to notice that Ava and J.P. were still kids, decades later. George Washington, meanwhile, had taken the bobblehead from J.P. and was studying it carefully.

"Quite a likeness, Vice President Adams!" George Washington said to John. Ava agreed. John looked about the same age as the bobblehead at this point.

"Yes, quite, quite," John said, getting that look of false modesty on his face again.

"It's from the John Adams Visitor Center," J.P. proclaimed. George Washington gave John a quizzical look, and the bobblehead began nodding and bobbling.

Then Ava and J.P. were back at the wedding dinner. Her head was spinning. Seeing Sam appear and then disappear. Talking to George Washington and attending his inauguration. The fact that George Washington really did have J.P.'s Star Wars ship. It was all too much.

"Man, oh, man," J.P. was saying to Chloe and Nathaniel. "You guys really missed out this time! George Washington was there too! And of course he remembered meeting me that other time. I guess I'm pretty unforgettable!"

Nathaniel shook his head. "I'm not sure I believe any of this," he said skeptically.

"It really might be one of those apps," Chloe said, echoing her brother's skepticism. "Virtual reality and all. Or maybe you two are just delusional!" She smirked at Ava.

"This isn't an app!" Ava said, infuriated. "And I'm not delusional! It's real! They really were there, and so were we!"

The music was softer now, and people were starting to leave. J.P. yawned loudly, and Ava found herself yawning too. Her mom and Steve and Grandpa Ed were heading toward their table, along with Chloe and Nathaniel's parents.

"Must we leave now?" the bobblehead asked. "I see your families are approaching. I, for one, would rather stay! This wedding has been most exhilarating!"

"Well, we can't leave you here," Ava said, as the adults descended on them. As she hugged Aunt Suzanne and Uncle Patrick and put on her jacket, she kept thinking about time travel. Would she end up running into someone else she knew if she kept going back in time? And why couldn't Sam see or hear them?

In the car on the way back to Grandpa Ed's apartment, the bobblehead began grumbling in its box. "Please take me out," it implored. "I would like to see my surroundings."

Ava, sitting in the back seat next to J.P., saw that he had fallen asleep, so she pulled the bobblehead out of the box and sat it on her lap so it could see out the window. Grandpa Ed had tuned into a classical music station and the bobblehead seemed to approve, nodding and bobbling its head.

"Do you understand the rules of time travel?" Ava asked it quietly, so Grandpa Ed wouldn't hear.

"If I did, would I tell you?" the bobblehead said, sounding annoyingly like J.P. "But in truth, I do not. It's extremely complicated!" And it nodded and bobbled some more.

"Do you think there are other kids out there traveling back and forth to different time periods? Like us, and like Sam?"

"Oh, I dare say!" the bobblehead said, nodding and bobbling enthusiastically. "Now where are we? Do you know?"

Ava looked out the window. They were crossing a

bridge over a river. "I'm not sure. This might be the Charles River," she guessed.

"Ah, yes. It all looks so different from my time," the bobblehead said. "These tall buildings, all the lights at night. What happened to the peace and quiet? A moonlit night with only the sound of the animals in the distance?" It paused and gazed out questioningly.

"See, Ava, we're passing Harvard now," Grandpa Ed said from the front seat.

The bobblehead began nodding and bobbling again. "Be this Harvard College? No!"

"Apparently, yes!" Ava replied, looking out into the night at a series of red-brick buildings. She had walked around Harvard Square, with its shops and restaurants, with Grandpa Ed on several occasions, as it was near his apartment.

"But I attended Harvard College," the bobblehead said. "And it looked nothing like this!"

Ava refrained from saying that of course it would look different more than 250 years later.

"I was but fifteen years of age when I started at Harvard," the bobblehead continued. "Not much older than you."

"I'm only ten," Ava said. "I'll be eleven in January, though." She couldn't imagine going off to college in five years.

"Precisely," the bobblehead said, nodding and bobbling. "At age ten, my son John Quincy accompanied me to France. He was extremely capable. At fourteen, he was employed as the translator and secretary to another diplomat."

Ava found this remarkable. Clearly, kids had to grow up a lot faster back then.

"Of course, it was difficult for my children with me away doing the business of the government," the bobblehead said. "Mrs. Adams raised the children mostly by herself, except when they went on diplomatic missions with me and Mrs. Adams stayed at home."

Sounds familiar, Ava thought.

"A bit like your own situation," the bobblehead said, eyeing her shrewdly. "Of course, I don't think either of your parents are serving the government." And it preened a little.

"Well, no," Ava said. "But my mom's a therapist, and she helps people, and my dad's a vet, and he helps animals."

"What, pray tell, is a therapist? And a vet?" the bobblehead inquired.

As Ava began to explain her parents' work, Grandpa Ed parked the car and shut off the engine, and J.P. stretched and yawned.

"Ah, yes, the new veterinary science," the bobblehead was saying. "Fascinating, yes."

Ava was about to explain that it wasn't new, but perhaps to the bobblehead it was. She'd have to ask her dad when veterinary science became an official thing.

"Where are we?" J.P. said, stretching again and hitting Ava in the face.

"Ow!" she cried. "You hit me in the face!"

"Sorry!" J.P. said. "Next time, move your face!" And he started laughing.

"Okay, enough, you two," Grandpa Ed said, escorting the two of them into the apartment.

J.P. promptly fell asleep once they were in their beds, but Ava tossed and turned. The wedding, the inauguration, the bobblehead, all the momentous and strange occurrences of the past two days swirled around in her head, causing a mental commotion that would not allow sleep to come.

She heard the bobblehead muttering something in its box.

"What?" she whispered.

"Bunker Hill!" it said. "We never made it to the end of the Freedom Trail!"

Why was the bobblehead so fixated on Bunker Hill? Ava's thoughts turned back to Abigail. She vaguely remembered something about Abigail and Bunker Hill from her report.

And suddenly she was somewhere else again. It was no longer dark, so clearly she was not in Grandpa Ed's guest room. And she no longer heard the gentle snores of J.P. across the room and the mutterings of the bobblehead, but instead a distant thumping noise. Fireworks? It reminded her of the Fourth of July.

As she adjusted, she saw two figures near her. This seemed familiar somehow. Hadn't she experienced this before? Who was it?

"Mamma, I know Pappa would want us to view this," a boy's voice exclaimed.

"It is important to be here, Johnny," came a woman's voice. Abigail? John Quincy? She looked toward them. Yes, it was Abigail and John Quincy, but they were unaware that she was nearby.

The distant booming continued, and Ava felt the same sense of unease creeping over her that she had experienced the previous day. Something or someone was missing, and she was supposed to figure it out.

"Your dear pappa told me to take all of you and fly to the woods, but I felt it was important for at least some of us to witness this," Abigail continued. She sounded agitated. What exactly was going on?

"I know I will remember this day for the rest of my life," John Quincy said in a quavering voice. He was a kid again, probably around J.P.'s age, not a teenager. Was this 1775? 1776? "The cannon, Mamma!"

Cannon? Is that what the booming sound was? Was she somehow in the middle of a Revolutionary War battle? She tried desperately to remember what she had written in her report, but the details kept slipping away. Instead, a feeling of dread hit her. Someone was missing. And it was her fault.

The cannon boomed again, and Ava screamed. She opened her eyes and found herself in Grandpa Ed's guest room. Had it been a dream? Why did she keep returning to that moment? And what exactly was her fault?

"What?" J.P. was shouting from across the room.

"What? What?" Half-awake, he jolted up in bed and stared at her. "Why were you screaming?"

"I wasn't screaming," Ava said, trying to hold onto her dignity. "Maybe you dreamed it!" And she turned away, hoping she would be able to fall asleep and have peaceful dreams.

Chapter ~6~

va was busy writing in Just Putrid the next morning when Chloe burst into the guest room, followed more slowly by Nathaniel.

"Watch out!" J.P. screeched from the floor, as Chloe trod heavily upon one of his Legos. "What the . . . you broke my police vehicle!"

Chloe ignored him and settled down on the bed next to Ava. Nathaniel sat on the room's one chair, which was covered with dirty clothes.

"Whatcha writing?" Chloe said, leaning over. Ava slammed Just Putrid shut.

"Nothing!" she said quickly.

"Oh, your diary," Chloe said, drawing out the word "diary" in a sing-songy way. "I guess you're busy writing all about your visit with John and Abigail Adams, even though we all know it wasn't real."

Nathaniel nodded. "They're some kind of imaginary hallucination," he said. "I've been looking up more stuff about it. Sometimes there can be mass hallucinations, where everyone believes something that's not real."

"This is not a mass hallucination," Ava said.

"Certainly not!" the bobblehead huffed.

"Then maybe you're writing about your boyfriend," Chloe taunted. Ava could feel herself blushing. She didn't have a boyfriend. There wasn't even anyone she liked.

"Shut up," she said. Not a great comeback, but what the heck.

Nathaniel looked up from his phone and snickered. "Burn," he said. "Good one, Chloe."

"That was not a burn," Ava said indignantly.

"What is a burn?" the bobblehead inquired.

"You know, like a 'gotcha' type of thing," Ava explained.

The bobblehead nodded. "I am sure that whatever you are writing in your diary, young lady, is most fascinating!" it said.

"Oh, it is!" J.P. said, before clapping his hand over his mouth again. "I mean, I'm sure it is!"

Ava glared at him. "If you look at it one more time . . ." she began.

"Writing is one of the true pleasures in life," the bobblehead continued. "Of course, there were all the letters Mrs. Adams and I wrote back and forth in the years we were apart. And then there was my correspondence with Mr. Jefferson. Quite a surprise, that was." He started nodding and bobbling.

"Ava's a really good writer," J.P. said. "She won a writing prize last year!"

That was true. She was surprised J.P. remembered.

At the time, he had seemed far more interested in Star Wars. Ava's mom had made her favorite dinner the night Ava won the prize, a special chicken dish with vegetables, and her favorite chocolate cake. It had been delicious. Ava sighed with the memory.

"Well, I won three prizes last year," Chloe said. "One was for math, one was for reading, and one was for being the best flute player. Right, Nathaniel? I won the most prizes of any fourth grader in the whole school."

Nathaniel, glued to his phone, grunted.

"Ava's prize was for the whole county, not just for our school," J.P. retorted. True again. Not that Ava wanted to boast about it or anything. And since when was J.P. her cheerleader? It was puzzling. Nice, but puzzling.

"How wonderful, young lady," the bobblehead said. "Keep up the writing. All of you should do that." He looked around at them. "One can get distracted, especially with all the newfangled things you carry around with you." And he gestured at Chloe and Nathaniel's phones.

"So what happened between you and Thomas Jefferson, anyway?" Ava asked. She remembered something about a feud, and that they became friends again in their old age. And they had died on the same day, July 4, 1826, fifty years after Independence Day. But she didn't want to mention that to the bobblehead. It seemed morbid.

"Ah well, we were friends, and then we went our separate ways, and then we rekindled our friendship," the bobblehead said, its eyes misty. "Such wonderful letters we would write back and forth. Of course, we both were in our later years and were not as involved in affairs of state as we had been."

Ava nodded. The scene from last night, the dream—or had it been?—flashed through her mind. She shivered a little. It had been so strange.

"Why do you keep talking about Bunker Hill?" she asked the bobblehead.

"An important battle," the bobblehead said. And that seemed to be all it felt like saying. For once it was silent.

"Are you leaving today too?" Chloe asked. "We're going to the airport right after the brunch. We only have a short flight back to New York, and we both have soccer games in the evening. Our teams can't manage without us. I usually score most of the goals."

Ava, who had yet to score a goal after five years of soccer, wondered if this could possibly be true. Could a person really be that good at reading, math, flute, *and* soccer? Her mind focused on a girl at school named Macy. She was incredibly mean, but was really good at everything. One time she had tried to start a rumor that Ava was moving to California permanently. "Good riddance," Macy had said. And a couple of the other kids had laughed. Ava thought Macy and Chloe would probably get along well. She needed to discuss this with Samantha when she got back home.

"We're leaving later this afternoon," Ava replied. They were supposed to gather for brunch back at the hotel. Ava loved brunch. She hoped they had pancakes. She just hoped she didn't have to sit next to Chloe. Or Nathaniel. Or J.P.

Back when Ava's mom and Steve had gotten engaged, and Ava realized that Steve and J.P. would be moving in with them and that J.P. would be her stepbrother, she had sat on Samantha's bedroom floor after school and cried.

"Having a brother's not so bad," Samantha had said, patting her on the back and trying to reassure her.

"But Brian's older than you, not younger," Ava had sobbed. "And he's your real brother. And he's not annoying."

"Oh, yes he is!" Samantha had argued. She said J.P. was actually a pretty good kid, but Ava had glared at her and Samantha hadn't said anything more. Until a couple of weeks ago, that is, when Samantha was over and the three of them ended up playing soccer together down the street across from Samantha's house, and it hadn't been that bad. J.P. had said some things that were even a little bit funny, and Samantha had commented on it later. But Ava had changed the subject.

The bobblehead, which had been uncharacteristically quiet, cleared its throat. "Returning to the subject of Mr. Jefferson," it said, "how happy it made me to have such a wonderful correspondent. Our letters brought great pleasure to my life, especially after the death of Mrs. Adams." A tear came to its eye.

Ava nodded sympathetically.

"Of course, there were issues upon which Mr. Jefferson

and I held quite opposing views. Slavery, for one. A terrible thing. Indeed, I feared that issue would split our country in two."

Well, he was absolutely right, Ava thought. It was a terrible thing, and the country did eventually split in two, during the Civil War. Was the bobblehead aware of this? How much did it know about what had happened after John Adams died? And why was it always silent during their trips back in time?

The bobblehead began nodding and bobbling again, and Ava held her breath. Where were they going this time? She closed her eyes against a rush of dizziness, and opened them to find Nabby looking at her, appearing to be about ten years old again. They were back in the front room of the John Quincy Adams birthplace.

"Why do you always appear so suddenly?" Nabby asked. "It gives me quite a start!"

Ava thought back to how Sam had suddenly vanished from the room after the inauguration, and had to agree. "I'm not exactly sure," she told Nabby. "But that's true, it is startling."

John Quincy and the two younger boys wandered into the room, along with J.P., who was holding the bobblehead.

"Did you remember our own toy?" Charles was asking. "The one like that?" He pointed at the bobblehead.

"Oh, no!" Ava and J.P. said together.

"The thing is, we're never quite sure when we're coming to visit you," Ava said, feeling terrible. When would they ever be able to give the Adams kids their bobblehead? She and J.P. were leaving Boston later that day. Would they still be able to travel back and forth once they were home in Maryland?

"How did the inoculation go?" J.P. asked, looking around at the kids. "Did it hurt a lot? Did you feel really sick?"

They looked blank and Ava realized they had landed in a time period before the summer of 1776.

"Which inoculation?" Nabby finally asked.

"Oh, nothing," Ava said, but J.P. piped up, "For smallpox!" She glared at him, hoping he would get the hint.

"What?" he said. "Why are you looking at me like that, Ava?"

"But we have not been inoculated for smallpox," Nabby said. The others murmured their agreement.

"May I?" John Quincy asked J.P., reaching politely for the bobblehead. J.P. handed it over.

"We do miss Pappa most awfully," Charles said, as the Adams kids gathered around the bobblehead. "He's in Philadelphia. Still."

Ava sort of wished she had a bobblehead of her own dad for all the times she was in Maryland and he was in California. But of course they could talk on the phone, email, text, Facetime, and Skype. All the Adams kids could do was write letters and wait weeks for a response, because back then the mail was slow between Boston and Philadelphia.

"I guess you can't call him, yeah," J.P. said thoughtfully.

"Pappa! Pappa!" Charles addressed the bobblehead, laughing. Little Thomas joined in.

"He surely couldn't hear us all the way in Philadelphia, no matter how loudly we called," John Quincy said sadly, and Nabby nodded.

"The situation in Boston grows worse, and Mamma is dreadfully concerned," Nabby said. "People are evacuating from the city."

"Why?" J.P. asked, pulling a stray Lego from his pocket.

"The war, silly," Charles said, looking at J.P. with surprise.

"Oh, right," J.P. said.

"What's that?" John Quincy asked, eyeing the Lego mini-figure curiously.

"It's the young Obi-wan Kenobi," J.P. said. The Adams kids stared at him as if he were speaking another language. "It's pretty rare, I think, or I'd give it to you. But you can hold it if you want." He handed it to John Quincy, who tapped it with his fingernail.

"What is this substance?" he asked.

"Plastic! Duh!" J.P. said, looking incredulous.

Ava rolled her eyes at J.P.'s usual cluelessness. Clearly, plastic hadn't been around back then, judging from the expressions on the Adams kids' faces.

Figuring that this might be an opportunity to get away from the ever-annoying J.P. and the other boys and talk to Nabby, maybe discuss some of the things they had in common, Ava drew Nabby toward a corner of the room.

"You know, I don't see my father very much either," Ava began. "He lives far away. I only see him during the summer and school vacations."

"Oh, dear," Nabby said, frowning. "How unfortunate! I am sure you write him many letters!"

"Well," Ava said. Did emails count? "We write frequently, yes."

"You must miss him," Nabby said, shaking her head sympathetically.

Ava did, but probably not the same way Nabby missed John. She tried to think what it would be like without having any contact at all. Not seeing her dad's face for months on end, or hearing his voice, would be awful.

"But it must be a comfort to have your stepbrother," Nabby continued. "He's in the same situation as you are, only seeing one parent at a time, right?"

"No!" Ava burst out. "He's not a comfort at all! And his mom lives ten minutes away! It's not the same thing!" She noticed the boys looking over curiously.

Nabby looked confused and a little hurt. "Oh," she said. "I know my brothers are a comfort to me, even when I find them most vexing. But this must be quite different, I suppose."

"I'm sorry, Nabby!" Ava said, suddenly feeling as if she might cry. "I didn't mean to get upset with you." She reached over and gave Nabby a quick hug. "It's just that, like, oh, I don't know." She didn't know what to say. Something about how J.P. wasn't her real brother, and why did her dad have to live so much farther away than most other kids' parents, and why did her mom have to get married again anyway? Steve wasn't so bad, and neither was Eleanor, certainly not like wicked step-parents in books. But still.

She felt some of her sadness lift when Nabby hugged her back.

"I understand," Nabby said, sounding as if she, too, might be near tears. "Sometimes I get very upset. Why did my father have to be the one to go to Philadelphia for months on end? When will I ever see him again?"

"What's with you two?" J.P. said, bounding over to them, holding the bobblehead. "Why do you look so sad? Why are you hugging each other?" Curious, the other boys circled around them.

The bobblehead began nodding and bobbling, Ava's head began pounding, the swirling feeling hit, and she was back in Grandpa Ed's guest room.

There was a knock at the door, and her mom came in. "Everyone doing all right?" she asked. "Ava? You look pale. Are you okay?"

Ava blinked a few times, trying to adjust. She rose from the bed, pushing past Chloe, who was on her phone. Skirting J.P.'s Legos, Ava ran over and gave her mom a big hug. "I'm okay," she mumbled. Her mom would never understand all the time travel stuff. She would just think Ava was tired.

Brunch was in a large room at the hotel with walls of windows looking out onto a brick courtyard. The weather was sunny, and light streamed in.

Ava tried to get a seat next to her mom and Grandpa Ed, but once again she ended up near J.P., Chloe, and Nathaniel. She couldn't understand why adults assumed that if they liked certain adults, the children of those adults would also be friends. If she ever had kids, she would not assume that. She would use Chloe and Nathaniel as Exhibit A.

"You went off again," Chloe said, stuffing a big forkful

of omelette into her mouth. "To the imaginary Adamses. Not that I missed you when you were gone."

So she had been gone? Or maybe Chloe just thought she was gone.

"The Adamses aren't imaginary!" Ava said, feeling frustrated. She poked at her pancake and wondered how Nabby felt when she, Ava, disappeared again. "They were real people and we actually visited them."

"Yeah, they were real people," Nathaniel said scornfully, waving his fork for emphasis. "Back in the eighteenth century. But these so-called visits are just hallucinations. They're not actually happening."

"Yes, they are!" Ava argued. She thought about how upset Nabby had been about her father. Certainly that was real. "Why do you keep denying it?"

"Yeah!" J.P. said. He pulled the bobblehead out of its box. "Hey, John! Can you explain this to them?"

The bobblehead shook its head, seeming sad. "There are those who do not believe," it said. "There is only so much I can do." It paused, brightening as it peered at J.P.'s French toast.

"And what, pray tell, is that?"

"French toast," J.P. said, his mouth full.

"Ah, yes!" the bobblehead said. "Of course, being part French, you would enjoy French toast." And it bobbled and nodded in a self-satisfied way.

"Actually, French toast wasn't originally from France," Nathaniel said. "It was probably from the Romans. We learned that at school the other day."

"Now, your father is not French, correct?" the bobblehead said to J.P.

"Correct," J.P. said. "My mom's the one who's French. Her family went there from Vietnam, like, a long time ago. My dad's a white American guy. Not French or Vietnamese. Here, try some!" He held a forkful of French toast, dripping with syrup, in front of the bobblehead.

A drop of syrup fell on its face, and it licked it up. "Delicious!" it said. "Thank you!"

"I know you can't really eat," Chloe said, picking up the previous day's discussion. "You're just a bobblehead, and bobbleheads can't eat."

The bobblehead began bobbling angrily. Its face began turning red. Uh-oh, Ava thought. It seemed to be working its way into a full-fledged tantrum.

"You're not built to eat," Nathaniel added. "You're made of material that doesn't allow for it. And why am I talking to you anyway?" He shook his head.

"Ignorance!" the bobblehead sputtered. "Impudence! Young people who don't know their place! My place was as president of the United States! I was the first one to live in the White House when it was new! You need to be taught a lesson about how important I really am!" And it began nodding and bobbling so much that Ava feared its head would fall off.

The windowed walls of the brunch room began to wobble and grow hazy, and Ava shut her eyes. When she opened them, she was in a room she had never seen before. It wasn't part of the John Quincy Adams birthplace, that was for sure.

John Quincy Adams
Birthplace

The room was large and, bizarrely, hung with household laundry—sheets, shirts, petticoats. As she adjusted to her surroundings, she heard a female voice mutter, "I would far rather be at Peacefield than here." Ava peeked behind a billowing sheet to see where the voice was coming from. And there was Abigail, fastening the laundry to some sort of hanging protrusion.

"One would think the president's house would be in better condition," Abigail said through a mouthful of clothes pins. "Hello again, young lady, a pleasure." She took the pins out of her mouth, hung up the cloth, and smiled at Ava. "But we must make do." Abigail looked older, her face finely etched with lines. Was this actually the White House? It certainly looked nothing like the elegant rooms Ava had seen in pictures.

"Where are we, exactly?" Ava asked.

"An audience room," Abigail said, sighing. "Or that's what it's meant to be. I use it for my washing, as you can see." She gestured at the laundry. "I was not sure what to expect here in Washington City," she continued. "I must say, I find the house freezing. We must keep thirteen fires going each day to stay tolerably warm. And I am most uncomfortable to see slaves at work." She pointed at a large window that looked out on a wintry scene. "Just outside here, around the corner, working away, removing large amounts of dirt. Would that our New England customs would prevail here." Ava nodded in agreement.

She looked around. Yes, this must be the White House, but clearly it was still a work in progress. The room was freezing and did not look finished at all. No beautiful furniture anywhere in sight.

Abigail picked up another sheet and handed one end to Ava. "If you wouldn't mind," Abigail said, skillfully spreading out the cloth between them and pinning it up. "This house requires thirty servants to run well," she said. "And we have but six."

This laundry-pinning was not what Ava imagined First Ladies doing. But before she could give it further thought, she heard familiar voices.

"I heard them!" J.P.'s voice came from somewhere

across the room, through the maze of drying laundry. "I know they're here somewhere."

He burst through a sheet, followed by Chloe and Nathaniel.

"Abigail!" J.P. said.

"My little friend!" Abigail said. "And you two." She looked at Chloe and Nathaniel, not seeming at all pleased to see them. Perhaps she was still upset that Chloe had called her a peasant and Nathaniel had poked John in the arm. And that they seemed to doubt her existence. That must really seem like an insult.

As if on cue, Nathaniel jumped in. "So where has our video game taken us this time?" he asked. Chloe snickered. Ava watched as they tried, unsuccessfully again, to take a picture of Abigail with their phones. Wouldn't they ever learn? Cell phones wouldn't work in whatever year this was. 1800, maybe?

"I know not what a video game is, but we are currently situated in the president's house," Abigail replied. "Please behave respectfully."

Chloe and Nathaniel started laughing. "How can we respect something that's fake?" Chloe said, and that set them off even more.

"Well!" Abigail huffed. Her eyes flashed. "I have had enough of your rudeness!"

"I'm truly sorry for their behavior," Ava said. "They don't seem to understand where they are." She glared at Chloe and Nathaniel, who were hiccupping with laughter.

"Yeah," J.P. said, also glaring at them. "Behave!"

"Abigail!" came a voice through the laundry. "Abigail! Where are you?"

John bustled toward them, moving sheets out of the way. "More trouble, Abigail. I fear this election will not go our way." John looked older too, maybe even older than the bobblehead, which J.P. was holding.

Ava tried to remember how the election had turned out. She knew John had been a one-term president. He had lost his bid for reelection in 1800. Thomas Jefferson, his vice president, had become president.

"'Tis frustrating, Abigail," John said, throwing his hands out in despair. "Mr. Jefferson has gone his own way, and Mr. Hamilton has also betrayed us." Alexander Hamilton? Ava wondered. A couple of kids she knew had seen the musical "Hamilton" and went around singing the songs.

"I did warn you, John, Mr. Hamilton is treacherous," Abigail said.

The bobblehead seemed agitated, perhaps at the thought of Thomas Jefferson and Alexander Hamilton? Perhaps at the prospect of losing the election of 1800? In any case, it started nodding and bobbling furiously. Ava tried not to look at it. She wanted to stay here and experience more of what was going on. But her head started to swirl, and of course, when she opened her eyes, the laundry and the White House were gone. There in front of her was her plate of half-eaten pancakes.

Chapter
~7~

Grandpa Ed, who believed in getting to airports early, dropped them off at Logan Airport at 2 p.m. for their 5 p.m. flight back to Washington. Ava hated the goodbyes at airports and train stations. It made her feel melancholy. She always waved until she couldn't see Grandpa Ed—or her mom, or her dad, or whoever it was she was leaving.

"Bye, Grandpa!" J.P. shrieked as Grandpa Ed's Jeep pulled away from the curb and joined the stream of cars exiting the airport.

"Bye!" Ava whispered. She knew he'd visit them soon, but she still felt like crying. Ava's mom put her arm around her.

"We'll see him again in a couple of weeks," her mom said, as they hoisted their backpacks on their shoulders and wheeled their bags into the terminal. "And we can call him tonight."

Well, goodbyes weren't all bad, Ava thought, remembering Chloe and Nathaniel. They had bid each other farewell after brunch was over.

"It's been wonderful meeting you!" Chloe and Nathaniel's mom had said, hugging Ava and J.P. "Now that we're all related, we hope we'll see you often!"

"Yes," Ava said, gritting her teeth as Chloe smirked from behind her mom's back.

"Step-cousins by marriage!" J.P. had proclaimed. "I think I've figured it out!"

The adults beamed at J.P.

"So smart!" Ava heard someone say.

"And he's only eight!" another voice said.

Aunt Suzanne, looking chic in her usual black— she was an art teacher—had swooped over to Ava's side. "You were a fabulous flower girl," she said, embracing her. "And a great clarinet player too! I'll have to sneak you into my suitcase when Patrick and I go to Hawaii." This was a game the two of them had played over the years. When Ava was little, she had often tried to get into one of Aunt Suzanne's suitcases.

A honeymoon in Hawaii. Ava could almost hear Nabby sigh, "How romantic!" It was. Definitely more romantic than going back home to Bethesda. As she and her mom, Steve, and J.P. stood in the security line, she wondered again if, now that she was going home, the bobblehead would still be able to take them back in time. Maybe its time-travel ability declined the farther it was from its own home. What if she never saw Nabby again?

J.P. had been chattering to Steve about Legos, but he suddenly looked panicked when they reached the security gate. "I can't put John through the metal detector!" he whispered to Ava. "He'll freak out! He'll start to yell and scream and then we'll all be put in jail!"

He had a point. She didn't want to imagine what would happen if the bobblehead ended up in prison. "Let me talk to it," she said.

"Come on, kids," Steve said, loading their luggage onto the conveyor belt to go through the scanner.

Ava had to act quickly. J.P. pulled the bobblehead box out of his backpack and handed it to her. "Listen, John," she said, whispering into the box. "You're going to have to go through a sort of tunnel, okay? So just be quiet and don't start to yell or anything."

"Take me out of here!" the bobblehead commanded. "Where am I?"

"Ava!" her mom said, placing her keys and shoes in the tray. "We need to get everything on here now!"

"Okay," Ava said, feeling frantic. She leaned over the box again. "We'll take you out in just a couple of minutes, if you can manage to be quiet. All right?"

She could hear an angry snort coming from the box. "As I've said time and again, I am perfectly capable of remaining quiet when I choose to, young lady!"

Well, that was probably about as good as she would get. She pushed her backpack and clarinet onto the belt, then helped J.P. put the bobblehead back into his pack and send it through the scanner.

She thought she heard muffled grumbling as she stepped through the metal detector, but the uniformed agents—all adults, of course—didn't notice, much to her relief.

Once through the scanner, J.P. took the bobblehead out of its box. "See?" he said, as they headed for their gate. "That wasn't so bad, was it?"

"Where was I? What was that contraption?" the bobblehead spluttered, turning to look back at the security apparatus behind it. "Well, I never! Travel has become so complicated! When I left the White House for the last time, I headed out in a simple public stagecoach. Leaving the nation's burdens to Mr. Jefferson." And it snorted again.

"There's the gate!" J.P. yelled, pointing down the hallway. "See? B-14!" He started running toward it.

"We're, like, three hours early," Ava called after him. "You don't need to run!"

"Hey, Nathaniel!" J.P. was shouting. "Nathaniel! Chloe!"

Ava's heart sank. She thought she had seen the last of them at the restaurant. Ava's mom and Steve were smiling and waving. Indeed, there at the gate next to theirs were Chloe, Nathaniel, and their parents, waiting for the flight to New York. Chloe and Nathaniel were on their phones. They waved half-heartedly.

"What are the odds of that!" Steve was exclaiming.

"Gates right next to each other!"

What indeed? Ava wondered. She checked the board to see what time the plane was leaving. Three-fifteen p.m. An hour and forty-five minutes before their own flight to DC. Well, at least that was something. "What time is it?" she asked.

"Two-thirty," her mom said. "You know how Grandpa Ed likes to get to airports early."

J.P. sat down next to Nathaniel, dropping his backpack with a sigh. Ava could see that her mom and Steve were settling in for a lengthy chat with Chloe and Nathaniel's parents. All she could do was hope that Chloe and Nathaniel's flight started boarding soon.

The bobblehead's head was nodding and bobbling. "All that running!" the bobblehead said. "It's left me quite out of breath."

"You weren't running, he was," Chloe said, pointing at J.P. "Can you even run?"

"It can't run," Nathaniel said, rolling his eyes. "Jeez, Chloe!"

"Of course it can," Ava said loyally. "If it chooses to."

"Quite right, young lady," the bobblehead said, nodding and bobbling more vigorously.

J.P. sighed again. "This trip has been so fun," he said. "And tomorrow I have to go back to school." He turned to the bobblehead. "Can you make it so I don't have to go to school anymore?"

The bobblehead shook its head. "Did I ever tell you about the school I attended as a boy? I absolutely hated it! And I told my father that I'd much rather be a farmer. Work with him on the farm."

"That sounds kind of fun," J.P. said, perking up. "Maybe I could help him too!"

"I later concluded that it was the teacher I found objectionable, rather than school itself," the bobblehead continued. "As you know, I became a most successful student." It smiled happily. "As I'm sure all of you are." It looked around at the four of them, nodding and bobbling. Ava closed her eyes and felt her head pounding, and when she opened them, she was sitting on a porch. Vines were growing up its pillars. It looked familiar.

Also seated on the porch were J.P., Nathaniel, Chloe, and two elderly people in old-fashioned clothing. She squinted at them.

"Who are those old people?" J.P. said loudly.

"Shhh!" Ava said, mortified.

"When is he arriving?" the elderly woman asked. "It must be quite soon now!"

Wow, it was Abigail, Ava realized, recognizing her voice. So the elderly man must be John. And this was the porch of Peacefield, the house they moved into when they returned from Europe. Ava had seen it on the tour. The weather was warm. The trees were leafy and the grass was green. It must be summer. But what year?

"What the heck?" Nathaniel said, recognizing them too. "They've really aged a lot!"

"Who are they?" Chloe asked, poking her brother. "Where are we?"

"It's our young friends," John said, getting up creakily from his chair and walking over to extend handshakes to Ava and the others. "A pleasure! We are welcoming John Quincy home today." Abigail smiled and nodded from her chair.

"Oh," Chloe said. "We're back to this again. But they're old now."

"Yeah," Nathaniel said. "These special effects are amazing. I don't get why my phone never works when this happens. It's so weird."

Ava sighed. "Where is John Quincy coming home from?" she asked John and Abigail.

"All over," John said, waving his hands in the air. "The Netherlands. Russia. Prussia. Great Britain. It has been years since we've seen him. We are to have a party for him tonight. Come in, we will show you the house."

He helped Abigail from her chair, and the two of them walked slowly inside, the children following. John and Abigail took them through what looked like a dining room and then into a very large room, which she remembered from the tour. You could probably fit the entire John Quincy Adams Birthplace into this one room, Ava thought. Clearly this house was much fancier than their previous one. They all settled into the upholstered chairs.

"John Quincy has been named secretary of state," John said proudly.

"'Tis truly the next most important post next to the president himself," Abigail added. "Who knows, perhaps one day he will follow his father into that role."

"Yes, he will!" J.P. said excitedly.

John and Abigail smiled, the you're-so-cute look spreading across their faces. "We appreciate your confidence in our son," Abigail said, reaching over and patting J.P. on the head.

Just then, a younger woman rushed into the room. "They're here! They're here!" she cried. Ava could hear a commotion outside. John and Abigail hurried as fast as they could to the porch, and the rest of them followed.

A stagecoach pulled by four horses had stopped in front of the house, and dust was flying. Two teenagers and a boy about Ava's age jumped out. "Oh, Grandmother!" one of the teenagers cried, racing over to Abigail. A man and a woman emerged. Ava barely recognized John Quincy, but surely that's who it was, accompanied by his wife. There was a round of embraces and tears of joy.

The bobblehead was caught up in the emotion too, Ava noticed. It was nodding and bobbling with excitement, and tears were trickling down its face. Ava felt as if she might cry too.

"Hey!" Nathaniel said suddenly, interrupting Ava's moment of joy. "We're going to miss our plane!"

"Oh, man," said Chloe. "And what about our soccer games?"

Ava couldn't help being a little pleased about the idea of Chloe and Nathaniel being inconvenienced. On the other hand, if they missed their plane, she'd have to spend more time with them in the airport. She took the bobblehead from J.P. "Please, get us home," she said, bobbling it gently. It seemed to get the idea, because a minute later, they were back in the airport terminal, where a line of people snaked toward the boarding gate. "Last call for the flight to New York's LaGuardia airport," a voice said. "Please report to your gate immediately for boarding."

"Where were you?" Chloe and Nathaniel's mom cried. "We looked everywhere!"

"We were so worried about you!" Ava's mom and Steve chorused in unison.

"Don't ever do that again!" Chloe and Nathaniel's dad added.

"We probably won't," Nathaniel said, picking up his backpack. "Not if we can help it. Bye, guys." He waved to Ava and her family. Her mom and Steve were on the verge of a giant lecture, she could tell.

"If you get any photos of so-called John and Abigail, please send them," Chloe said. "Oh, that's right, you don't have a phone. Bye!" She and Nathaniel snickered.

"Burn!" he said as they disappeared through the door.

Ava heaved a sigh of relief. She looked down at the bobblehead. It still looked emotional, and there was still a hint of tears on its cheeks. "I'm sorry to take you away from such a nice experience," she told it.

"Ah, well, it can't be helped," the bobblehead said. "But it was wonderful to relive that day. It was in August of the year 1817, by the way," it said. "I could tell you were wondering."

"Thanks," she said, giving it a little hug.

Sure enough, Ava's mom and Steve launched into a reminder about safety in public places. They were right, Ava knew, but time travel had a way of interfering.

"We need to be able to see you at all times," Steve concluded.

"Okay," Ava said. J.P. nodded, as did the bobblehead.

"We were so scared!" her mom said. "One minute you were there, and the next . . ."

"I know," Ava said. "We won't do it again." At the same time, she was curious. So when they went back in time, their parents just couldn't find them? Did they suddenly disappear? And did time pass as quickly, or slowly, in the present as it did in the past?

"You'll stay right here," Steve said, gesturing at the row of black vinyl seats next to them. There weren't many people around, as their flight still wasn't due to leave for quite a while.

Ava and J.P. settled into their seats. Reassured, Steve started leafing through a magazine, and Ava's mom opened her book.

"Apologies, apologies," the bobblehead said to Ava and J.P., shaking its head. "I did not mean to cause anxiety to your parents! As a parent myself, I can sympathize greatly with their feelings."

"Does this mean we can't go anywhere any more?" J.P. said, looking dejected. "Isn't there something you can do?"

"Like make them so interested in whatever they're reading that they don't notice anything?" Ava suggested. "They both like to read, you know."

The bobblehead put its hand to its chin. "Hmm,"

it said. "I will see what I can do." It seemed to think for a while, and then it snapped its fingers. "Yes, yes, of course! Bunker Hill! Of course, most of the battle actually took place on Breed's Hill, but so it goes." And it started nodding and bobbling vigorously. Before Ava could ask why it was so fascinated by Bunker Hill, she blinked and found herself back in the front room of the John Quincy Adams Birthplace, with J.P. next to her.

The distant booming sounded oddly familiar.

Where had she heard that before?

"What's that noise?" J.P. asked. "It sounds like a battle!"

The Adams kids ran down the stairs. "We thought we heard someone!" Nabby said excitedly. "The cannons have been firing for hours now! Mamma is quite concerned."

If the bobblehead had chosen to take them back to the Battle of Bunker Hill, perhaps that was what they were hearing. Wasn't that the first big battle of the war? How far away was it? Ava wasn't sure.

"Did you bring us the toy that looks like Pappa?" John Quincy asked. "Remember, you showed it to us yesterday?"

Yesterday? Had one of their visits occurred just the previous day in eighteenth-century time?

"You remember," Nabby said helpfully. "Mamma was writing to Pappa about pins?"

"Of course!" Ava said. How strange that she and J.P. would turn up the very next day, but without the second bobblehead. "I'm so sorry! We really will get it to you soon!"

The Adams kids seemed momentarily disappointed, but then another boom startled them.

"How far away is Bunker Hill?" Ava asked. "Or Breed's Hill, or wherever this is going on?" She hoped it wasn't too close.

"Perhaps ten miles or more," Nabby replied. "We know not what will happen if the British are victorious."

She shivered despite the day's warmth.

Abigail came breathlessly down the stairs. "Your dear father would not advise us to do this, but I feel we should witness history." She paused to greet Ava and J.P. "You are here on a momentous day," she said. Ava and J.P. nodded. "Johnny, you will accompany me," Abigail said to her oldest son. "I believe Charley and Tommy are too young, so Nabby, you will stay here with them."

"But where are you going, Mamma?" Nabby asked.

"I shall go to the top of Penn's Hill," Abigail responded. "It's close by, and we should be able to get a view of what is happening. It's not possible to just sit by and be so completely uninformed! Come, Johnny. We shall be back soon, Nabby, Charley, Tommy." She quickly embraced the three of them and ushered John Quincy out the door.

"Come on, let's go!" J.P. said, nudging Ava. "I want to see the battle!" Ava felt bad leaving Nabby behind with the little kids, but she wanted to follow Abigail.

"Go ahead," Nabby urged Ava. "Please do come back soon and tell us what is happening!"

Ava and J.P. rushed ahead to catch up with Abigail and John Quincy. "Ava, will you hold the bobblehead for me?" J.P. asked. Soon he and John Quincy were deep in conversation. Each of them had picked up a big stick and were dragging the sticks along and poking each other, leaving Ava to walk with Abigail.

"So much commotion," Abigail said. "Mr. Adams

has been gone for so long and will be gone for months more, it seems. This war will doubtless go on for quite a while."

Ava knew the war had lasted years and years, but she couldn't remember exactly how many. "Yes, quite a while," she echoed.

"And I do hope that in the future, the ladies of the colonies are given a voice," Abigail continued. "The Congress, you know, consists entirely of men, and I feel that if ladies were involved in the business of the day, things would be accomplished in a far more effective manner." Ava nodded in agreement.

Abigail waved briskly to some other people walking down the hill. The cannons continued to fire, but the group still couldn't see them. "Sometimes I think men would be tyrants if we let them," Abigail said. "I have a mind to write this to Mr. Adams one of these days. Remember the ladies!"

"You certainly should," Ava said. She knew Abigail had followed through on that idea. It was one of her more famous letters, perhaps the most famous one. "You will be seen as a champion of women's rights!" Ava said.

"Do you think so?" Abigail said. "Well, perhaps I will then." They were approaching the top of the hill. John Quincy and J.P. had run on ahead, and as Ava glanced at them, she noticed a strange glowing object next to John Quincy, like what she had seen near Thomas Jefferson. Was it the same thing? She shook her head

to clear her thoughts. This was just too weird. She could see the glowing shape turn toward John Quincy and J.P. It seemed to wave at J.P., who batted it away. The glowing shape seemed to want to talk to J.P., but then it turned around and bounded down the hill toward her.

"What is that?" Ava asked in a quavering voice. "That glowing thing coming toward us?"

"I see no glowing thing," Abigail said, peering ahead. "Perhaps you are seeing some smoke from the battlefield? We are almost high enough to see what is happening." Ava felt winded, but Abigail pressed on determinedly. The shape was closing in, and it was taller than Ava. It reached toward her as if to shake her, but when she screamed, it retreated toward John Quincy.

They had reached the top of the hill now, and far in the distance, smoke was rising from a site that seemed miles away. The cannon noise was louder. Ava suddenly realized that she was witnessing— although from afar—an actual battle. People were probably being killed. She started shaking.

Abigail seemed agitated too. "Terrible, terrible," she said, blinking away tears.

John Quincy rushed over, also in tears. "Mamma, I know Pappa would want us to view this," he exclaimed, his voice shaking.

"It is important to be here, Johnny," Abigail said. "Your dear pappa told me to take all of you and fly to the woods, but I felt it was important for at least some of us to witness this." The conversation sounded oddly familiar, Ava thought.

"I know I will remember this day for the rest of my life," John Quincy said. "The cannon, Mamma!" The blobby glowing figure next to her nodded as if to agree.

Ava clutched the bobblehead and looked out at the dark smoke coming from what she assumed was Breed's Hill. John Quincy and Abigail and the blob were looking too. And then Ava suddenly realized that someone was missing. J.P. was nowhere to be seen.

Chapter
~ 8 ~

He must be here somewhere. Ava glanced around from her vantage point at the top of the hill and tried not to panic. "J.P.!" She turned to the others. "Have you seen J.P.?" It was like that dream she had the other night. Someone had been missing.

"He was right here!" John Quincy said. "Right next to me!" The blob nodded.

"J.P.!" Ava yelled. The cannons boomed again and she shivered. Where was he? Could he have wandered off toward the battle? It was far away, but maybe he would have tried to get there anyway? "J.P.!"

The others started calling his name, and Ava grew increasingly worried. J.P. had absolutely no common sense. What if he ran into a British soldier and insulted him by mistake? Or confused him with some twenty-first-century reference, and then the soldier took offense? What if he ended up in an eighteenth-century British military prison? Or worse?

"Johnny, do you know any places where he might be hiding? Or a path he might have taken?" Abigail asked.

John Quincy thought for a minute and then ran off, the blob following. Abigail set off in another direction to look for J.P.

Ava turned to the bobblehead. "Can you think of a path he might have tried to take?" The bobblehead nodded and gestured toward yet another direction. Ava headed that way, but soon began to feel lost. The terrain was bumpy, and she tripped over a tree root and banged her knee. "Ow!" she cried, picking herself up and looking around. "How am I ever going to find him when I have no idea where I am?"

The bobblehead pointed back in the direction of the hill. "Yes, it wouldn't be good for me to be lost too," she said. "One of us has to be able to figure this out!" She thought of Steve, and J.P.'s mom, and her own mom, and how upset they would be if J.P. disappeared. She should have kept a better eye on him. She had been distracted by the glowing blob, and then J.P. had vanished. An image of him wandering into some battle scene, holding a Lego, popped into her head, and she sighed.

Despair settled over her, and she sat down

on a rock. She remembered a story her mom had told her, about how when Ava was really little, the two of them had gone to the library and her mom looked away for a minute, and Ava was gone. Frantic, her mom had called her name for what seemed like forever, and enlisted the help of others. Ava turned up a few minutes later, quite unharmed, having run around an entire block. Ava had never understood why her mom was so panicked. Now, she did. Not that J.P. was really little, but he was still kind of young to be off on his own in a whole different century during wartime.

A few minutes later, Abigail and John Quincy returned to the top of the hill, out of breath. "No sign of him," Abigail said, raising her palms in defeat. "Johnny?"

"Nothing," John Quincy said. He was followed by the blob. "I searched in some of my favorite hiding spots."

"Perhaps he returned to the house." Abigail suggested. "We could all go back and see."

That made sense. Ava ran to the John Quincy Adams Birthplace ahead of the others and burst through the open door.

Nabby was waiting. "What did you see?" she asked eagerly.

"Have you seen J.P.?" Ava asked.

"No," Nabby said. "Why, has he gone missing?"

Ava felt a growing sense of panic. "I think so," she said, on the verge of tears. If J.P. wasn't at the house, and he wasn't up on the hill, where was he? And she had the bobblehead, so he couldn't have gone back to the twenty-first century without it, could he? She pulled the bobblehead out of the box just as Abigail and John Quincy reached the house.

"He is not here?" Abigail asked Nabby, who shook her head. Charles and Thomas emerged from the back room. "Are you sure you haven't seen him?" she asked them. Maybe the three of them were playing hide-and-seek. But the boys looked serious and insisted that they hadn't seen him since he had left to go up the hill.

Ava went out to the front porch to think. She knew the bobblehead didn't talk when they were time traveling, but she thought maybe it would in an emergency.

"Do you know where J.P. is?" The bobblehead shook its head. People were rushing up and down the main road. She could overhear snippets of conversation about the battle and the cannons and the British.

The bobblehead seemed upset too, and started bobbling frantically. "Can you take me back home, I mean, to the airport, and see if he somehow went back there?" It nodded and bobbled, and a minute later she was sitting in the vinyl chair at the departure gate.

There were her mom and Steve. "Oh, hi, Ava!" her mom said, looking up from her book. "Only about twenty minutes now until we board!"

"Hey, Ava!" Steve chimed in, glancing up from his magazine.

"Where's J.P?" her mom asked.

"He's over there," Ava said, gesturing vaguely to the left. As they returned to their reading, she chose a seat a few chairs away.

"Where could he be?" she asked the bobblehead urgently.

"I can tell you that he's not here in your time. He's back in my time," the bobblehead said. "He couldn't have come back here without me." And it preened a little.

"But I have to find him!" Ava said, teary-eyed. She was the older one. She had been responsible for him. She imagined him wandering around by himself in the eighteenth century, and near a battlefield, no less. What if she never found him? Would he grow old there and end up becoming some famous bilingual person, the age of her great-great-great-grandfather to the tenth power? That was too weird to contemplate. She took a deep, shaky breath.

"We shall go back and look," the bobblehead said, on the verge of tears itself. "We shall scour the area." It looked over at their carry-on luggage scattered near Ava's mom and Steve. "Get my fellow bobblehead from your backpack," the bobblehead said. "I might need reinforcements."

"Good idea," Ava said, and she grabbed the box containing the second bobblehead. Her mom and Steve smiled at her and kept reading.

"Okay, let's go," she said. The bobblehead began nodding and bobbling, and a minute later they were back on the road in front of the John Quincy Adams Birthplace. She opened the door, which creaked slightly, and went in.

"What a horrible day, first witnessing the battle and then J.P. going missing," John Quincy said. "Mamma has gone 'round to the neighbors to see if they have seen him. Being a visitor, he might be quite lost."

Ava nodded. That's what she was worried about. And she knew her mom and Steve would start to panic when boarding began and they realized their children were gone. She gulped back a sob.

"Oh, Ava!" Nabby said, appearing next to her. "How thoughtful of you! In the midst of looking for J.P., you brought us the figure of Pappa? Thank you!"

"Yes," Ava said, handing over Bobblehead Two as the Adams kids gathered around. She whispered, "Thanks!" to the bobblehead. She never would have remembered to bring Bobblehead Two if he hadn't suggested it.

Ava stepped outside with the bobblehead to continue her search for J.P. and found the glowing blob waiting around the corner. "What do you want?" she asked. "Who or what are you, anyway? I need to find my stepbrother, okay?"

The blob nodded, bobbling around like the bobblehead, which also was nodding and bobbling. Ava started to feel queasy. "Please, both of you, stop it!" she cried. "We need to find J.P., now!"

The blob shrugged and made talking motions. But how could it be talking? The bobblehead, meanwhile, was quiet. But it was watching the blob, which continued its gesturing and started up the hill again. Ava followed. Perhaps this glowing object had some idea where J.P. had gone. After all, it had been with John Quincy and J.P. at one point, and then it had distracted her, and then J.P. had vanished.

Oh, no. Another thought popped into her head. "Could J.P. have gone into some other time period entirely?" she asked the bobblehead. "Like, maybe the Middle Ages? Or, say, the Civil War?" The blob tilted its head, considering this, while the bobblehead put a finger thoughtfully to its chin. After a minute, it shook its head decisively.

Just then, Nabby came out of the house, holding the second bobblehead. "Mamma is back home again, and the neighbors have not seen J.P.," she said. "I shall help you look."

"Nabby," Ava said, "Do you know what that is?" She gestured at the blob.

"Why, of course," Nabby said, matter-of-factly.

"Really?" Ava said, surprised. "What is it?"

But just then, Bobblehead Two began to stir. "Where am I?" it asked creakily. Nabby jumped. "It talks!" she said. Ava realized that because the original bobblehead hadn't talked when it was visiting the past, Nabby hadn't experienced a talking bobblehead. "And it does sound quite like Pappa!"

"Actually, this one talks too," Ava said. "Sometimes I can't get it to stop talking."

"Also quite like Pappa!" Nabby said, smiling.

"I believe the young visitor has gone that way," Bobblehead Two said, pointing up the hill, where the blob was already heading. By this point, it was way ahead of them.

"Mr. Adams!" the original bobblehead said, nodding at Bobblehead Two. Ava was surprised to hear it talk in this time period, but figured it didn't want to be outdone by its counterpart.

"Mr. Adams!" Bobblehead Two said, nodding and bobbling back. "I believe our young visitor has gone up the hill. Or rather, that he stayed up the hill. Mrs. Adams is often right, but her belief that the young visitor went back to our home is clearly incorrect."

"On that, Mr. Adams, I would have to agree," the original bobblehead said. "Yes, Mr. Adams."

"Yes, Mr. Adams, we are as one on this," Bobblehead Two said, and they started nodding and bobbling and talking in stereo. Nabby watched in amazement.

Ava, meanwhile, was growing impatient. "Come on," she said. "If you both think he's still up on the hill, then what are we waiting for?"

"Talking toys!" Nabby said. "Most extraordinary!" Ava pulled Nabby along, while their bobbleheads tried to out-talk each other over the sound of the cannons.

As they reached the top of the hill, the original bobblehead peered around. "Please lift me higher, young lady," it ordered. "I need to get a better view."

"And the same for me, Nabby," said Bobblehead Two. They looked to and fro, nodding and bobbling excitedly.

"The battle seems most intense, Mr. Adams,"

the original bobblehead said.

"Yes, it does, Mr. Adams," Bobblehead Two said. "As we were in Philadelphia at the time, we were not able to view it closely."

"Yes, Mr. Adams," said the original bobblehead. "And the descriptions provided us by Mrs. Adams were quite thorough and most moving, although a trifle overwrought."

"Yes, Mr. Adams," said Bobblehead Two.

"Although Philadelphia has its good points, Mr. Adams, we much prefer Boston. Fie on the British who are damaging our city, Mr. Adams!" said the original bobblehead. "Fie on them!"

"Yes, Mr. Adams!" Bobblehead Two agreed. "Fie on them!" And they nodded and bobbled vigorously.

Ava was about to lose it. "Please stop talking!" she said. If she heard them say, "Yes, Mr. Adams" one more time, she would scream. Although she had to admit that "fie on them" was a pretty good expression. "We need to find J.P.! Do you see any sign of him from up there?"

"Perhaps Andrew . . ." Nabby said, but her words were lost in another roar of distant cannon fire.

"What? Andrew who?" Ava realized she sounded rude, but time was growing short. "Our friend," Nabby said. "Our other friend, I mean. The one who went up the hill ahead of us."

So the blob had a name: Andrew. How bizarre, Ava thought. But no stranger than anything else that had been going on this weekend.

"Do you see this Andrew anywhere?" Ava inquired. "Perhaps it, or rather, he, has been able to figure something out."

"Andrew!" Nabby called. "Have you any news?"

The blob appeared from behind a tree. It started gesturing again and waving its arms. "Oh, that way?" Nabby said, apparently perfectly able to understand what the blob was saying.

"I can't understand a thing it says," Ava said, curious despite the urgency of the situation. "How do you understand it?"

"I understand Andrew perfectly, just as I understand you," Nabby replied.

Remarkable, Ava thought. Maybe being able to understand glowing blobs was a special talent that eighteenth-century kids had. Well, it was best to play along. "So Andrew wants us to go that way?"

"Exactly," Nabby said. The girls and their bobbleheads followed the blob around a grove of trees and down a slight incline.

Nabby slapped her forehead. "Of course," she said. "It's a hiding place my brothers and I discovered long ago. We haven't been here in years! Perhaps Andrew discovered it on his own during one of his visits. I should have thought of that! Thank you, Andrew!" The blob gave an "it's nothing" shrug and led the way toward a small indentation in the hillside, where several rocks had been pushed aside. There, lying in the grass, was J.P.

Ava shrieked. Was he . . . had something happened to him? She leaned in, and when she heard him breathing, a wave of relief hit her and all the tears she had been holding back poured out in a torrent. "You're here! You're okay! You're here! You're okay!" It was all she was able to say.

J.P. stirred and opened one eye. "Ava? Where are we?"

"You must have fallen asleep! I couldn't find

you! None of us could find you, except that blob over there." Ava pointed behind her, but the blob was gone.

"J.P.!" Nabby said, also crying with relief. "We are so glad to find you. Andrew had to leave, but he said he thought you might have wandered off here. And there you were! I should have thought of this."

"Oh, Mr. Adams, a happy ending!" the bobbleheads said to each other, nodding and bobbling and weeping a little.

J.P. got up and brushed away stray bits of grass as Ava gave him a huge hug. J.P. hugged her back. She felt as if a gigantic weight had been lifted. Nabby jumped in and hugged them too.

"You are crushing us!" the bobbleheads said. The cannons sounded again, and the five of them rushed down the hill toward the John Quincy Adams Birthplace.

Ava wished she could thank the blob, but she didn't know where to find it. She'd ask Nabby later. "How did you end up there?" Ava asked J.P. "And how could you fall asleep with all those cannons firing?"

"I wanted to get closer to the battle," J.P. said. "You know, like the time with Sam and George, when I was right in the middle of it." Ava was glad her mom and Steve, and J.P.'s mom, had no idea of any of this. They would not have approved. "And then I must have gotten really tired, and I fell asleep."

When they reached the house, Abigail and the boys made a fuss over J.P. And in the midst of all the excitement, Ava realized that their flight was probably boarding and their parents were wondering where they were.

"Thank you all so much for everything," she said. "I hate to run, but J.P. and I need to get back home now."

"Of course," Abigail said graciously, and Nabby and the boys nodded. "We shall see you soon, no doubt?"

"I certainly hope so," Ava said, and she and J.P. held up their bobblehead. "Goodbye, Mr. Adams," it said, nodding at its fellow bobblehead. "A pleasure."

"Goodbye, Mr. Adams," said Bobblehead Two. "Likewise." And as they nodded and bobbled, Ava felt the dizziness hit, and then she was back in the airport on the black vinyl chair.

A voice came over the loudspeaker: "Now boarding all passengers for our flight to Washington, DC." Ava looked over at a line of people boarding the plane. Her mom and Steve were still reading contentedly, but Ava noticed the bobblehead bobbling in their direction, and suddenly their heads snapped up.

"Oh!" Ava's mom said, slipping the book into her bag. "Look, Steve, we're about to miss the plane."

"You're right," Steve said, putting his magazine away. They both looked dazed.

"Come on, Ava, J.P.," Ava's mom said. "Let's get in line."

"Thank you both for staying right here," Steve said. "That's a big help!"

Ava, J.P., and the bobblehead looked at one another. "What they do not know will not hurt them," the bobblehead whispered, and Ava and J.P. nodded. "I am most delighted that you were found, young man," the bobblehead said, turning to J.P. "I must confess, I do not understand how one can fall asleep in the midst of a battle, but so be it."

"I guess I didn't get too much sleep last night, so I was tired," J.P. said. "Ava was screaming in her sleep. Sharing a room with her is kind of a pain." Ava felt a flicker of annoyance seep through her newfound tranquility, but she pushed it aside.

She had too many questions to ask him. "So do you understand who this blob was that helped us find you?"

"Oh, John Quincy's friend?" J.P. said. "The shiny one? I couldn't see him very well, but John Quincy said he was their friend. Arthur, I think?

Or Aaron? Something with an A."

J.P. didn't seem fazed by any of this. "Andrew," she said. "So how did he know where you were?"

J.P. shrugged. "I have no idea!" he said happily. "But I'm glad he found me before the plane boarded. Our parents would have been really mad!"

As they walked toward the plane, J.P. said, "Ava, will you sit next to me this time? I want to tell you about these cool Legos that are coming out. I have the catalog, so I can show them to you."

Ava considered this offer as they waited in the jetway. "Okay," she said. At least he couldn't kick her seat if he was next to her.

They settled into their seats and J.P. pulled out the Lego catalog. Ava thought about John and Abigail and Nabby and the boys. She reached into J.P.'s bag for the bobblehead and took it out of its box. "Will we ever get to see them again?" she asked it. She held her breath waiting for the answer. "And what about that blob?"

The bobblehead looked around. "Another modern conveyance?" it said, eyeing the airplane cabin skeptically.

"Yes, it's a plane. It's going to take us 30,000 feet up into the air, and then an hour or so later, we'll land in Washington, DC, I mean, Washington City, as you would call it. And your ears might pop a little with the altitude change," Ava said. Might as well give him all the information.

"Fly? In the air? Like a bird?" the bobblehead said, nodding and bobbling. "I once witnessed a balloon flight. In Paris. With Mrs. Adams and Mr. Jefferson. Quite fabulous it was, yes, yes."

"But will I get to see Nabby and the others again?" Ava persisted. She really had to know. The plane pulled away from the gate and started taxiing out to the runway.

"Look, Ava!" J.P. poked her a couple of times. "It's the new set of Star Wars ships." He pointed to a page in the catalog. The poking kind of hurt, but Ava didn't mind. Oddly enough, she was glad to have J.P. sitting on the plane next to her showing her his Lego catalog, instead of trapped in the eighteenth century with no way home.

"Nice," she said, before turning back to the bobblehead. "So what do you think?"

"Legos are a most fascinating invention," the bobblehead said, nodding and bobbling. "Yes indeed. And . . . oh, my heavens! This conveyance is going way too fast! Aieeeeeeeee!" And it let out an enormous, panicked shriek as the plane took off, gained altitude, and headed over Boston Harbor.

Ava looked around, wondering if a flight attendant would come rushing over. Of course they didn't hear the bobblehead's screams, though a few kids nearby glanced over curiously.

"This is incredible!" the bobblehead said, calming down. "Lift me up a little higher, young lady, so I can see out this porthole." The plane made a wide turn and headed out over the ocean. "This is far superior to the first ocean crossing I made with John Quincy." And it nodded and bobbled contentedly.

"So what do you think?" Ava repeated. "Will I get to see Nabby and all the others again?"

"Time will tell!" the bobblehead said. It smiled and turned to the window to enjoy the view.

Testimonials

"If novels are the narrative form of play, then Deborah Kalb's new book, *John Adams and the Magic Bobblehead,* is like a really great recess — fun, active, and an excellent way to learn a little about yourself and the world around you."

—Jill Vialet, founder and CEO of Playworks and author of *Recess Rules.*

"Time travel at its best. Join Ava and J.P. on a jam-packed journey back to the days of the American Revolution, walk along the Boston Freedom Trail, and peek inside the President's House in the new capital of Washington. While John and Abigail Adams share historic milestones and words of wisdom, it's contemporary family relationships (and sibling rivalry) that are at the core of this amazing adventure. Deborah Kalb keeps readers spellbound and has them laughing out loud just as she did with *The President and Me: George Washington and the Magic Hat.*"

—Kem Sawyer, author of *DK Biography: Abigail Adams*

"Deborah Kalb has written a dizzying, exhilarating romp through history with John Adams as a spirited bobblehead — yes, the same John who adores his independent Abigail, hates being stuffed in a toybox, and always has grand ideas about the future of his country. A perfect choice to spark an interest in important Americans who usually seem far-removed and boring."

—Karen Leggett Abouraya, author of *Hands Around the Library: Protecting Egypt's Treasured Books*

"A spirited talking souvenir, in the shape of a John Adams bobblehead, makes for a whimsical time machine in this fun tale of ten-year-old Ava and her eight-year-old stepbrother J.P. Like the figurine's bobbling head, Deborah Kalb's narrative moves between the eighteenth century and the present day. The story captures Ava's struggles to become part of a blended family: at the same time she experiences first-hand what life was like for Adams and his family as the United States struggled to be born. The conflicts of those two worlds merge, and Ava's feelings for her new brother transcend time."

—J.H. Diehl, author of *Tiny Infinities*

About the Author

Deborah Kalb is a freelance writer and editor who spent more than twenty years working as a journalist. Long interested in history, she is the author of *The President and Me: George Washington and the Magic Hat*, and the coauthor, with her father, Marvin Kalb, of *Haunting Legacy: Vietnam and the American Presidency from Ford to Obama*. Deborah lives with her family in the Washington, DC, area.

About the Illustrator

Robert Lunsford has been a graphic artist/illustrator for nearly forty years. A graduate of Virginia Commonwealth University's School of the Arts, Rob spent his career as a graphic artist at Roanoke, Virginia's daily newspaper. Recognized by the Virginia Press Association, Society of News Design, and American Advertising Federation, Rob is known for his ability to tell stories through pictures and information graphics. He is married to a fellow artist and teacher and has two grown children.